STEP BROTHER 10

with *Benefits*

SECOND SEASON

MIA CLARK

ISBN: 1517294363
ISBN-13: 978-1517294366

Book design by Cerys du Lys
Cover design by Cerys du Lys
Cover Image © Depositphotos | avgustino

Cherrylily.com

DEDICATION

Thank you to Ethan and Cerys for helping me with
this book and everything involved in the process.
This is a dream come true and I wouldn't have been
able to do it without them. Thank you, thank you!

CONTENTS

ACKNOWLEDGMENTS

Thank you for taking a chance on my book!

I know that the stepbrother theme can be a difficult one to deal with for a lot of people for a variety of reasons, and so I took that into consideration when I was writing this. While this is a story about forbidden love, it's also a story about two people becoming friends, too. Sometimes you need someone to push you in your life, even when you think everything is fine. Sometimes you need someone to be there, even when you don't know how to ask them to stay with you.

This is that kind of story. It is about two people becoming friends, and then becoming lovers. The forbidden aspects add tension, but it's more than that, too. Sometimes opposites attract in the best way possible. I hope you enjoy my books!

STEPBROTHER WITH BENEFITS

1 - Ashley

'M KIND OF HORNY. I know this isn't exactly the best time or place for this, because it's morning and it's light outside, but it's still early, right? I don't actually know, and I can't check my phone or a clock because we don't have them here. I hadn't really thought about that before now, but it's becoming increasingly more frustrating with each passing second.

Ethan said that phones don't work out here very well and they don't get much signal, but I could at least use it to check the time because I'd sort of like to seduce my stepbrother. He's sleeping, though, so this is going to be difficult.

Is it *actually* difficult? I've done this before, but not the same way as how I'd like to do it now. We've slept together basically every night for the past week. Um... actual sleeping, I mean. We've uh... we've *slept* together quite a bit more than just every night, but that's something else entirely.

One time I accidentally made him cum in his sleep, though. I just wanted to touch him and hold his cock, but that kind of led to me stroking him slightly, and before I knew it Ethan's cum was covering my fingers and he was still sleeping next to me. Oh, and then yesterday when I was teasing him, but he woke up before things went too far and we didn't get to finish that, so I'm not sure if it counts.

Now, though...

He's still asleep, so I think maybe it's early? Early is good. It's bright out, though, so it can't be too early. If I'd been awake to see the sun rise, this would all be much easier, but I wasn't. I don't hear our parents moving around or talking outside, so they must be asleep, too.

I'm still wearing the lingerie I wore last night for Ethan, but he's basically naked. He really should have put his pajama pants on before falling asleep. What if his dad catches him like this? Now I'm just being paranoid for no reason. Why would his dad catch him? It probably won't happen, and also I can just cover him up if I need to so that no one can tell he's naked.

That's the main problem here. Ethan *is* naked, and he's also asleep, and just like most every other morning, he's got an erection. He's on his back right next to me and I couldn't see his cock at first but I wanted to, so I lifted away the top of his sleeping bag, and...

Yes, Ethan has an erection. His cock is pointing straight up, and it grew a little harder, twitching and throbbing as soon as I released it into the open air.

This is a bad idea. Why am I thinking about doing it then? Except maybe it's not a bad idea? No, it's definitely a bad idea. Calm down, Ashley. You don't have to do this.

No. I *need* to. I need to do this. I don't know why I need to do it, but somehow, somewhere in my mind, I have convinced myself it needs to be done. It's extra important, now or never.

How can I argue against that?

Is this what Ethan goes through when he's considering his bad boy things? Because what I'm about to do is completely not a good girl thing. It's a really really bad girl thing to do, actually.

I reach out and touch the tip of Ethan's cock with my fingers, gently feeling it. His cock bounces and throbs from the sensation of my light touch. There's a drop of precum on the head of his cock and I carefully tease it with the tip of my finger, then slide it around until his entire cockhead is glistening with his arousal.

Quiet and careful, I scoot close, getting on my knees. I turn and twist around, then stand up slightly and put one leg on the other side of Ethan's body. I'm above him now, sort of just hovering there. I bend my knees and lower myself a little, a little more, more and more. I'm close now, directly over him, and the only thing stopping me from lowering myself entirely onto his cock is the fact that I'm still wearing panties.

Should I do this? I can stop. I can lay back down and pretend none of this ever happened and that I wasn't trying to seduce Ethan in his sleep, but... no. I can't. I can't just stop now. It's impossible.

I pull my panties aside and look down, making sure I'm lined up right. I lower myself a little until I can feel the head of Ethan's slumbering erection pressing against my feminine folds. As soon as I'm sure that I can push myself completely down without stopping, I do exactly that.

I'm wet and aroused and very ready for this, so it isn't exactly hard to do, but it takes a second for everything to fully sink into place, both mentally and physically. Then it's done, though. Ethan is inside of me. I press my hands down against his bare chest and squeeze tight against him, feeling his cock pulse and throb deep within me.

Ethan is sleeping, or he was sleeping, but he's very much awake now. His hips buck up, bouncing against me. I almost fall off of him from the power of his sharp thrust, but I steady and balance myself with my hands on his chest. His upper body jerks up, too, and his eyes shoot open. He looks confused at first, but not for long.

"Oh, *fuck*," he says, practically growling at me. His hands grab my hips and hold me down, pulling me onto his cock. "Good morning to you, too, Princess."

I whimper and grind against him, pressing my clit hard against his muscular body. He flexes inside of me, then flexes even more. It feels like he's about to cum, and I know it's easier to make him cum when he's asleep, so I think maybe he's going to. I don't mind, really. It's kind of sexy in its own way, sexy to know that I made him do that. Ethan scrunches up his eyes and looks like he's concentrating for a second. After a moment his erection stops twitching and flexing, but I can't feel his cum inside of me.

"No fucking way am I going to miss out on enjoying your tight little body," he says. "We had some fun last night, but now that I've had a chance to rest up... yeah... hope you aren't too tired, Princess."

I bite my bottom lip and grin at him, which I guess he takes as a challenge. He wraps his arms around me, pulling me close, and he bites my lip, stealing it from me and claiming it as his own. Before I can protest or kiss him, he lifts his hips up and presses his cock as deep into me as he can. I let out a lusty gasp, unable to stop myself.

It's loud. Too loud. Oh my God, our parents are going to hear us, aren't they? Except, no, they're asleep. I think they're asleep. I don't actually know if they're asleep. I don't even know what time it is.

Ethan apparently doesn't care about any of this, because he pulls out of me slightly, then bucks his hips up, pushing hard into me once more. Our bodies clap together, the sound of soft and hard smacks echoing through our tent and the woods around us. Yes, um... just like that... smack, smack, smack *smacksmack...*

If he wasn't holding me close to him, I think I would have fallen off by now. Being atop Ethan is kind of like riding one of those electric bulls, except I think this is even worse because it's not only hard to stay on, it's hard to concentrate, which makes it even harder to stay on. I whimper and gasp and grab onto the back of his head and his hair, pulling at it. This only seems to goad him on further.

Oh my God, what have I done? I was horny and aroused and I thought this would be fun. It *is* fun. Very very fun. It's just, um... *too* fun? That's what this is, if that's even possible.

If we were back home, it'd be fun, except we aren't back home, and our parents are very close by, so...

I can't really hear much except the sound of my stepbrother's body smacking against my own, except then I hear the sound of a zipper unzipping, too. It's the tent. Not our tent, thankfully, but a tent nonetheless. Then Ethan hears it, too, and he slows down, the sound of our bodies smacking together getting quieter, barely audible now.

He doesn't stop, though. Oh no, of course not. I started this with my attempt at being a naughty girl, and Ethan's definitely going to finish it because he's nothing but a bad boy. Except, um...

"Ethan? Ashley?" It's my stepfather. He's not right outside the tent, but he's pretty close. "Are you two awake?"

Mia Clark

2 - Ethan

ET'S JUST SEE HOW OFTEN my dad can cockblock me, why don't we? I feel like this is the most recent in a long string of unknowing attempts at cockblocking me, but it's also the one that's most frustrating. Possibly because I'm ball's deep in Ashley's perfect fucking pussy at the moment and usually when he cockblocks me it's before we even got started.

Yesterday, though? Yeah, going to count that. Trying to say that I should leave Ashley alone so she can see how things play out with the camp-ground owner's son? Fuck that, and fuck you, Dad.

I mean that in a nice way. I still like my dad, even if he's got a reputation for cockblocking me. I mean, I sort of still like him, but a lot of things are pissing me off lately.

I should really just figure out a way to tell him. Why not now? I could do it fast. Just shout out to him, say something about how I'm busy having sex with my stepsister at the moment and could he please back the fuck up?

Yeah, it's kind of rude, and also it's my fault for getting into this situation right now. I guess it's actually Ashley's fault, but I doubt I can blame her. Fuck... you know how amazing it was waking up to the warm, wet feeling of her pussy wrapped around my shaft? Surprising as fuck, and I was confused at first, but still amazing.

Little Miss Perfect may not realize it, but apparently she's really good at what she does. When she puts her mind to something, she goes all out. I admire that about her. I guess it's easy to admire her when her mind is focused on figuring out creative new ways to have sex with me, though. How can anyone even complain about something like that? I'm not complaining, that's for sure.

Not about that, anyways.

If we don't respond to my dad soon, he's definitely going to get suspicious. Best case scenario is he goes away, but he's still going to be awake. Sex won't exactly be easy then. Worst case scenario is he unzips the tent to check on us and finds Ashley completely impaled on my cock.

I want to tell him about us, but I feel like that's probably the worst way to do it. I don't know for sure, but I just have a feeling, you know?

"What's up?" I say to my dad, while begrudgingly lifting Ashley up and sliding my cock out of her.

She pouts at me a little, and I briefly contemplating slamming back into her hard to wipe that bratty little pout right off her face, but nah. This isn't the time for that. I wish it was, but it's not.

"Is Ashley awake, too?" my dad asks.

She pouts at me even more. I don't know why you're pouting at me, Princess. This is your own damn fault.

"Hi," she says, soft and cute and a little shy. Yeah, not sure about that one. This girl acts shy sometimes, but I don't know if I believe it.

"You two want to come out and help me with breakfast?" my dad asks. "Your mother's going to get up soon, too, Ashley. She was grumbling at me when I told her it was time to wake up, but I think the smell of bacon can convince her."

Fuck. Bacon? Yeah, my dad doesn't play fair. Also, I kind of want some bacon. I kind of want to finish what I was doing before he rudely interrupted me, but bacon sounds amazing, too.

"Sure," Ashley says, a smile on her face. Then she looks over at me and frowns. She reaches out with one hand and pats my cock like she's apologizing to it.

"Yeah, I'll be right out," I tell him, too.

"Alright," my dad says. "I'll get everything ready."

And that's it. We're sort of alone again, except my dad is right outside the tent. I can hear him opening the back of the car and then he's digging through the cooler of food we brought and rummaging through other stuff, finding all of our morning breakfast supplies.

"Do you think we can...?" Ashley asks, whispering, sparing a glance at my still throbbing cock.

"Look, Princess," I whisper, telling it to her straight. "I seriously want to lay you down on the ground and fuck the shit out of you right now, and then fuck you again afterwards for good measure, but we have all of a minute before my dad starts to get suspicious about why we aren't out there yet, and I doubt either of us can do all that much in a minute."

She sighs and pouts a little more. Fuck, what's with the pouting? Seriously, it's making me hard, which is quite the feat considering I'm already hard as fuck.

"Sorry," she says to me, sneaking in quick and kissing me. Then she says the same thing to my cock. "Sorry," she whispers, leaning close enough to kiss the tip. Her tongue languishes, tracing a line from the center, to the outside, then all the way around.

She's not sorry. No fucking way is she sorry. She's not even remotely sorry, because here she is almost giving me a blowjob, and... holy fucking shit.

She cups my balls in one hand, squeezing them a little, then parts her lips and goes all the way down my cock as far as she can, just taking me in her mouth, no big deal. This is kind of a big deal, Princess. Do you have any idea what you're starting here?

Instinctive, completely forgetting what I said before, I grab the back of her head and grip her hair in my fingers while she bobs up and down on my cock. She keeps going, just doesn't even fucking stop. I don't know if I love her or I hate her right now. Maybe a mix of both.

Aw yeah... take it, Princess. This is nice. I could do this all fucking day, except we don't have all day. We've got like... what, a minute or two?

Nah. Not even that.

"You two coming?" my dad asks. He's pretty fucking close to the entrance to the tent again.

Cockblocked again? Are you serious, Dad? It's Ashley's fault again, too. I don't think she realizes how much she torments me. It's beautiful fucking torment, but this shit is still torturous as fuck.

Ugh. Whatever. I'm done.

She bobs back up, and I just kind of lay there, defeated. I didn't cum. I've got a huge fucking erection throbbing between my legs and I didn't cum and I'm supposed to go out and help my dad with breakfast?

Fuck this shit. That's all I've got to say right now: Fuck this shit.

Ashley kisses the head of my cock again and whispers another apology to me, then she just slinks away, nothing doing, grabs her regular clothes, and slips them on fast. I lay there, on my back, with half a mind to just jerk off and finish this quick so I don't have to go through the pain of an unfulfilled sexual encounter. Also, how the fuck am I supposed to put my shorts on with what's throbbing between my legs?

Fuck if I know.

3 - Ashley

ETHAN SOMEHOW MANAGES to get his shorts on, despite the fact that his erection doesn't look like it's going away any time soon. I grin and try not to laugh, but it's hard. He grins at me, though, and gives me a look like he's going to show me exactly how *hard* it is later.

When we step out of the tent, he's mostly back to normal. I can see a faint outline of his shaft through his shorts, but they're loose enough that it's not too obvious. His dad is working on lighting a fire and doesn't seem to notice much of anything except that we're finally out and about. My mom joins us soon after, and we all make breakfast together.

It's kind of strange, though? It's not strange that we're all together, but cooking breakfast over a campfire is an entirely new experience for me. I'm not sure what I expected, but it wasn't this. It seems more communal in a way. It reminds me of when my mom and I cooked together back before she married Ethan's dad.

We lived in a small apartment with just a regular sized stove and a microwave to cook with. One of the burners on the top had burnt out and we didn't have enough money to pay for someone to fix it. Honestly it wasn't a huge deal, because we had three more burners on the stove, but it was one of the bigger ones so it was sort of almost impossible to cook anything in two big pots or pans at the same time. The smaller burners were alright for some things, but if we wanted to cook a big meal we ended up having some issues.

I never minded, though. We just couldn't always cook stuff evenly, and when we finished one dish and set it aside to start on the next, inevitably the first was a little cool by the time we were ready to eat. The microwave solved most of our problems, but reheating is never really the same as fresh, piping hot food.

That all changed when we moved in with Ethan and his dad, though. The concept of a stove burner that doesn't work was completely foreign to the both of them. Also we have two full-sized stoves now, both right next to each other. Plus a million other things to cook with. A rice cooker, rotisserie, side grill, a fryer... there's a lot more, but those are the things we use the most.

Now, though, it's just the campfire, and the four of us. It's kind of fun and I really like it. It reminds me of when my mom and I used to playfully fight for space in our cramped apartment kitchen while cooking together.

Ethan and I sit sort of side by side around the fire while my mom and dad sit next to each other, but closer. We're in lawn-style chairs that Ethan and his dad packed sometime yesterday for this very reason. It's cozy and nice, and the crackle of the fire is warm and inviting.

Ethan's dad sets up this grill sort of thing over the fire so that he can rest a pan on top of it, and we use that for eggs. It seems weird, but it works really well. We cook our own bacon on skewers, kind of like how we cooked the hot dogs last night. It's a little harder to skewer bacon on a stick, but it works fine and it's fun. I like how it's really fresh and you can cook it as crispy as you want.

I laugh when Ethan cooks his bacon just barely long enough to make sure it's cooked. He eats it as soon as it's safely done, not bothering with crispiness or anything. Then he gets more.

"Something funny?" he asks me when he's finished his third piece of bacon and I've barely finished cooking my first and just started to skewer my second.

"You sure are hungry, huh?" I say.

"I need to keep my strength up," he says, smirking. "I've got a lot of plans for today that are going to require a lot of energy."

I blush and mumble something, looking away from him. What's he even mean by that? I think I know exactly what he means, but I can't just come out and say it, nor can I ask him. His dad seems oblivious to any of Ethan's sexual undertones, and my mom just shakes her head and sighs.

"Speaking of what we have planned for the day," my stepdad says. "You two want to do anything in particular?"

"What's there to do?" my mom asks, genuinely curious.

"Hiking?" Ethan offers.

"Yeah, there's that," his dad says. "We could go to the lake, too. The main lake area is busier, but there's a river that feeds into it that's nice. There's natural rock slides there, carved and smoothed down by the river over hundreds and hundreds of years. It's fun."

"Yeah, there's this one spot where you can jump off a twenty foot high cliff into the water, too. It's pretty cool."

"I think I'll leave the cliff diving to you, Ethan," my mom says, winking at him before turning to me. "What about you, Ashley?"

"Um..." This is a step, I think. It's a step in the direction of being slightly less of a good girl. Sort of, though maybe not exactly. "I kind of want to try the cliff jumping thing... if it's safe?"

"Yeah," Ethan says, smiling at me. "It's safe, don't worry. I can show you."

"Maybe we could ask Caleb to come with us?" Ethan's dad says.

Maybe we can just ruin the mood completely? I don't say this, and I don't think I'd ever say it, but that's really what happens. One second Ethan is smiling, talkative, cooking his bacon, and the next he's quiet, glowering at his dad, practically bristling. Ethan's dad seems completely oblivious and continues to focus on scrambling the eggs in the one pan we have.

He finishes the eggs and dishes them out to each of us. No one is talking now, and I think it's for an obvious reason, but we have food as an excuse to be quiet, too. We eat our eggs on paper plates with plastic forks. Ethan's dad takes out large slices of bread and starts to toast them in the pan, using the same bacon grease he used for the eggs to make sure they don't stick. The bread toasts nicely, but it also soaks up some of the oil, becoming partly fried, as well.

I get the first piece of toast, and I say thank you, but I feel weird about it. I think this is the first time that Ethan's dad suspects something is wrong. It's weird to me that he doesn't notice these things very easily, because I can see them pretty clearly, but I guess it's because Ethan and I are being quiet about our secret.

I'm not even sure how to tell him, either. I want to, and I know Ethan does, too, but honestly I don't know how. It seems so hard and impossible.

It's also not my job to do it. Ethan wants to be the one to tell him, and...

I want to support him in this. I really really do. I just kind of wonder what would happen if I did it? Would it be alright if I asked Ethan's dad if we could talk privately and then I just told him everything? Would he be fine with it? I don't know what he would think about it. I'm not anywhere near as close with my stepfather as I am my mother, which seems obvious, but the problem there is that Ethan's closer with my mom than he is his father, too. Maybe my mom is just easier to talk to. I don't really know for sure.

We finish eating, regardless. The food is good and it's fun to sit together and cook and eat. I didn't know exactly how it worked before, but this is how I thought camping would be. It's cozy and nice and intimate in a familiar and safe sort of way. The sun shines on us, bright rays sneaking through the treetops, and a gentle breeze swishes through the leaves, mixing with the songs of birds flying from branch to branch above us.

"We probably shouldn't be getting too far ahead of ourselves," Ethan's dad says once we're finished eating. "We've got plenty of time to enjoy the great outdoors, but we should look into getting some food supplies while we're here. Maybe some fishing bait, too?"

"There's a grocery store, right?" my mom asks.

"Kind of," my stepdad says. "It's a lot smaller than what we've got back home. More locally grown food, though, which is nice. It's quaint, but it should have everything we need."

"Do you want to go food shopping with me, Ashley?" my mom asks, smiling.

I smile back at her and nod. "Sure, that sounds fun."

"Maybe you two boys can find something to do while we're gone?" my mom says, looking from Ethan to his dad, then back again.

Ethan mutters something and shrugs. His dad looks at him--actually looks at him now, and I think he's seeing something or someone he's never really seen before.

"Yeah, I'm sure we can," Ethan's dad says, smiling a little. "Ethan, you want to check out the bait shop with me? We can find out more about what's been going on since we've been gone and see if we can plan some fun things for the ladies. How's that sound?"

"Yeah, I guess," Ethan says, shrugging. "Sounds alright. Fishing's fun."

Is this good? I don't know. I think my mom planned this, though. If it's Ethan and his dad together alone, and then me and my mom, it'll make it easier for everyone to talk to each other? Sort of... or that's what I hope.

"Is there somewhere to shower first, though?" my mom asks. "I'm not used to this! I'd really love to wash up some before we go anywhere."

My stepdad laughs. "Yeah, you remember the main office? Right by there there's some shower stalls and regular bathrooms. I brought a few rolls of quarters for everyone. I'm not sure how much it is now, but you just go in a shower stall, put some quarters in, and you've got yourself a nice shower for a few minutes. If you need more, feel free to add more, but try not to go crazy with it. Everyone shares the showers here, so you might end up with a line."

"It's just one shower?" I ask. That seems sort of restrictive, but I guess it's camping so it makes sense that it would be.

"There's a few," Ethan's dad says. "They're all right next to each other. You have privacy and the shower doors lock, but you might end up taking a shower with someone in the stall right next to you on either side."

"Yeah," Ethan says. "It's not like anyone can see in yours, though. They're pretty big stalls, too."

"Yeah. Nothing to worry about. Just takes some getting used to, I guess. At the end of the day, a shower is still a shower, though."

I do like showers... also, I have some plans. I don't know if these are good plans or not, but I have them, and I sort of want to do them.

That's what got me in trouble this morning, isn't it? If I already got into trouble, why not get into more, though?

I'm pretty sure this is how it starts. I'm beginning to understand Ethan's bad boy ways a little better.

4 - Ethan

MY DAD AND ASHLEY CLEAN UP by the fire while Ashley's mom goes to take a shower and I do some other stuff. I don't really have a plan in mind here, but there's always something to do when you're camping. I unload some junk that Ashley's mom wanted out of the car and put it between the tents. After that, I go grab my bag with my clothes in it and make sure I've got everything ready for my own shower. By the time all of that 's done and Ashley and my dad have our stuff cleaned up from breakfast, my stepmom is walking back.

I head to the showers with my bag and a roll of quarters. She smiles at me as we cross paths, her going back to the campsite and me walking away from it. Her hair is still wet and it glistens in the bright morning sun.

"I can't believe I didn't think to bring a hair dryer!" she says, grinning.

"Yeah, tons of places to plug it in out here," I say with a smirk.

She laughs. "A girl can dream, right?"

"I guess you could always see if there's an electric hand dryer in the bathrooms up there and stick your head under it?" I offer.

She laughs even more and slaps playfully at my shoulder. "Sure, you try it first and let me know how it goes."

We separate then, her going back to our camp-site and my dad, and me continuing on to take a shower.

It's weird, but Ashley's mom is so much easier to get along with compared to my dad. I don't really want to compare her to my mom, but I think this must be what it's like to actually have a mother, too. I think about it sometimes, and think about what my mom would say to me if she was still around. To be honest, it's kind of hard, though. It's hard to remember everything about her and everything I know is trapped in the framing of a little kid.

I really like Ashley's mom, though. I'm glad she's my stepmom. I guess it's weird, but I think my mom would approve, too. I think she'd be happy that my dad found someone again, even if it took him awhile to do it.

I don't really know what my real mom would think about me dating my stepsister, but whatever. It's cool. I think she'd be cool with it.

My dad, though... yeah, he's not making this any easier.

The entire way to the showers I think about how to tell him. Do I even want to tell him? Fuck if I know, but I feel like eventually I kind of have to tell him, don't I? It's just one of those things that's going to come out sooner or later. Like... fuck... what if Ashley and I get married? Pretty fucking sure my dad's going to want to be invited to the wedding.

How the fuck does that even work? Shit, this is complicated, huh? So, alright, the bride's father walks her down the aisle, but that would be my dad? What's the groom do? Does the mom walk him down the aisle? I don't think so. I think there's first dance shit or something.

Wait, what the fuck? Why am I thinking about marriage? Seriously, that's fucked up. I've been dating Ashley for barely more than a week. I need to chill the fuck out or something.

You know what would be easiest, though? Eloping. You don't have to worry about anything if you elope. You just sort of run off somewhere and get married without all that fancy shit and there you go. Pretty sure Ashley's mom would castrate me if I didn't let her go to her daughter's wedding, though. You know what ruins a honeymoon real fucking quick? Being castrated. Shit.

Yeah, so, anyways, shower. I'm there. It's basically the same as I remember it. I step into one of the shower stalls around back and hang my bag up on the wall opposite the showerhead, then close the door and start to get undressed. When I'm good and ready, I get a handful of quarters out of the roll and pop them into the timer.

A dollar for five minutes? Fuck yeah, let's splurge a little. Ten minute shower? Holy fuck, maybe fifteen? Don't go crazy here, Ethan, save some water for everyone else. I put in four quarters, turn the knob to start the timer, then toss in four more for another five minutes. I'll see how it goes from there.

That's the plan, at least. Apparently I'm really fucking bad at shower plans, though.

5 - *Ashley*

SECRETLY CONVINCE MY MOM to distract Ethan's dad for a second. This is all part of my secret plans, which, um... they're not very elaborate, but it's the simple plans that are the most effective, right? I read that somewhere once but I don't remember where, and honestly I don't even know if it's true or not.

This plan isn't going to take a whole lot of effort, I just need to be a little sneaky for a second, that's all. I slip into the tent Ethan and I are sharing and then grab my clothes for the day, plus my shampoo and conditioner and my toothbrush and toothpaste just in case. You can never be too careful, right?

My mom is still talking to Ethan's dad and distracting him for the time being, which gives me plenty of time to slip away. I hurry away from our campsite, jogging quick down the road. Once I'm out of view, I slow down a little. I can't go too fast, because that would ruin part of my plan...

It's a secret plan. Shhh! Don't tell anyone, alright?

I realize I'm walking a little too fast when I see Ethan up ahead. He's got his back to me, so he can't see me, but that's definitely him. I slow down so that I don't catch up and so that he won't see me. It would kind of ruin the secret if he did, which is the entire point of this.

I wonder when we can tell his dad everything? I'm not sure. His dad doesn't seem very receptive to the idea, to be honest. I can sort of understand some of what he's doing, and I kind of like that he's thinking about me? I just don't like the fact that he thinks I'd like to spend time with Caleb.

I mean, it's not like I don't want to spend time with Caleb, either, though. I just don't want to spend romantic time with him? I think that's it, except I don't even know. I'm going to be super honest for a second and say that I'm actually not entirely sure what to do with a boy if you're just hanging out with them. Basically all of my friends are girls, except maybe Ethan, and Ethan's not even really my friend anymore, is he? Do boyfriends count as regular friends, too?

He wasn't exactly my friend before this, and I think we only ended up hanging out because our parents got married. Also, he didn't hang out with me a lot or anything, but we were sort of partly forced to hang out. It was fun, though. I liked all the times we spent together, and I think Ethan did, too.

I blush, remembering the party he planned shortly after me and my mom moved in with him and his dad. Our parents were away for the weekend and then I blurted out at the end that I was mad I didn't get to kiss anyone during any of the kissing games, and, um...

That was the first time we kissed. That was my first kiss ever, too. It was kind of weird, but I liked it.

I don't even know why I'm blushing, because recently we've done a lot more than kiss. This morning we did a lot more than kiss! I just liked it, though. I really like that Ethan was the first boy I ever kissed.

I want to be a first for him, too. I guess I am already, since I'm the first girl he's ever really dated, but I want to be another sort of first. I don't know what yet. I'm going to have to ask him and figure it out.

Before I realize it, I'm at the showers. It's kind of a strange building. It's rectangular and set off to the side, though I can see the main office from here, too. It's got two doors close together in the middle of this side, both of which lead to a bathroom, one for men and the other for women. Spaced further apart, one to the left of those doors and one to the right, are larger doors that lead into the shower stalls.

The shower stalls are kind of huge! I don't know what I expected there, but, yup, they're huge. This is good. It's perfect for my plans.

I'm guessing there's showers on the other side of the building, too, but I watch Ethan go into one in front of me. He still hasn't seen me, which is good. It's a secret, remember?

He closes the door behind him and a few moments later the water turns on. The doors don't go entirely to the floor or the ceiling, so I can see his feet through the bottom sometimes as he walks from one end of the stall room to the other.

I look around quick, making sure no one's watching me, and then I hurry to the shower that Ethan went into and open the door. Thankfully he didn't lock it. I slip in fast and close it behind me, then lock it and run to the opposite side away from the water.

Ethan stares at me as I enter. He's completely naked from head to toe, with water cascading across his sexy, muscular body, just standing there, watching me.

As soon as he sees me, his cock twitches. Well, hello to you, too...

I wink at him and he smirks.

6 - Ethan

APPARENTLY THE SHOWER FAIRY has decided to visit me. What, you've never heard of the shower fairy? Yeah, I don't know, I think she's some sexy as fuck little nymph that sometimes decides to join you in the shower. Sort of like the tooth fairy, but for adults. I'm pretty sure I like what the shower fairy has to offer a lot more than what the tooth fairy gives you, though.

"What the hell do you think you're doing?" I ask, smirking at Ashley.

Good fucking thing I didn't lock the door when I came in, huh? I didn't think anyone would interrupt me when I had the water on, so I doubted it would have mattered, but it seems to have worked out in my favor.

"Oh, just showering," she says, coy.

"Oh yeah?" I ask. "You do realize there's like, what, four showers?"

"Really, Ethan?" she says, hands on her hips. "Haven't you ever heard of helping the environment? I'm trying to save water here. This is for a good cause."

"Little Miss Perfect Environmentalist, huh?" I say, smirking.

She tosses me a dirty look and sticks her tongue out at me. Yeah yeah, whatever. It's not like I'm actually going to kick her out. How fucking stupid would that be?

She didn't really think this through too well, though. The shower is on and despite her best efforts, her shoes are getting wet. Also, she's got socks on, too. I took all that stuff off before turning the water on and tossed it on the wooden bench opposite the wall with the showerhead so it won't get wet. Ashley hurries and throws the change of clothes she brought into my bag hanging on a hook on the wall, then rips off her shoes and socks and puts them on the bench.

Yeah, actually, you know what? If she's going to do a good deed, help the environment and all, I figure I should do one, too. It's only fair, right? I stride across the stall towards her, grab the bottom of her shirt, and rip it up and off her body in one smooth stroke. She was working on getting un-dressed on her own, so she just kind of stands there, surprised, mouth open, staring at me. My hands are wet, and now her shirt is, too, but what the fuck do I care? I toss it onto the bench with her shoes and socks, then reach around and unsnap her bra in one second flat.

The straps fall down her arms and the entire thing just drops to the floor after that. She stares at me, gaping, eyes wide.

"Ethan!" she says, pretending to be alarmed.

"Why are you still wearing clothes?" I ask her. "Hurry the fuck up and get naked."

She does. Yeah, that's it, Princess. I love how she's scrambling to get naked for me. Fuck, this is glorious. I don't help her with her shorts, because it's more fun to watch. She scrambles quick with the button and zipper, then pulls them down her legs fast and steps out of them. When she almost stumbles and falls, I reach for her and help her stay steady. Her panties come next and those come off even faster.

She throws her shorts onto the bench, but she surprises me by throwing her panties right at me. They cling to my face, blinding me for a second, and then a second after that I've got this girl's soft, warm, partly wet body clinging to me. She wraps her arms around me and presses tight against me, embracing me. I snatch her panties away from my face and fling them against the wall, where they fall and land in the pile of the rest of her clothes.

Fuck this. You know how much I hated getting cockblocked this morning? Apparently about as much as Ashley hated it. I don't even know when I got hard, but I am hard as fuck right now. She wiggles and moves, trapping my cock between her thighs. Aw yeah, holy fuck, that's nice.

I pull back a little, then thrust forward. My cock glides between her thighs just under her pussy, and when I press forward I grab her ass and pull her as close as I can. Her clit grinds against the center of my body and the top of my shaft. She squirms a little, grinding against me even more, too.

This is some crazy shit right here. This is like having sex except not actually having sex. Kind of like dry humping except we don't have any clothes on and also we're standing right under the shower now so we're anything but dry. Water crashes down against her body and mine, making us slick and wet. I move my hands from her ass to her upper back and squeeze her tight, feeling her slick, shining breasts against my chest. Her nipples are hard as fuck and I just kind of want to bend down and pop them in my mouth, then roll them around with my tongue.

I don't get a chance to do this. This is not what Ashley has in mind. This is her surprise plan, so I guess I'm just kind of along for the ride at the moment. Don't worry, I'm not complaining.

She slides away from me, which is easy considering we're both wet and getting wetter by the moment. I try to grab her and keep her close, but the water covering her smooth body makes it hard and it's easy for her to escape me. She doesn't go very far, though. Doesn't even really go any-where but down.

When she's kneeling in front of me, almost on her knees, she grabs my cock and strokes it fast. Once, twice, and third time's the charm, I guess. Before the fourth stroke, while I'm reeling from the sudden sensation, she takes my cock in her mouth. Just like... for real, all the fucking way. Holy fuck, this girl's a freak.

Her beautiful lips wrap around my shaft and work their way down. I'm in heaven. Yeah, I told you the shower fairy is way better than the tooth fairy. You didn't believe me before, did you? I know what the fuck I'm talking about, alright?

She bobs up and down on my cock. I'm con-siderate, though. I'm a real good boyfriend here. I shift to the side so water doesn't spray in her face and then I put my hands on the side of her head, protecting her from any stray splashes. It's not because I want to pull her all the way onto my cock or anything. I mean, yeah, I kind of want to do that, too, but she's doing her own thing right now, and I'm certainly not complaining.

Her hands reach behind me and grab the back of my thighs. This is when I know it's serious, because her left hand means business. Her right is holding my leg regularly, but the left is loose, and it doesn't take me long to realize it's because she's squeezing her thumb and it's just the back of her fingers pressed against my thigh.

Oh, fuck. I don't even...

Seriously, for real, she means business. I look down at her and she's looking up at me. I almost lose it right there. Her eyes are wide, watching me, looking determined and innocent as fuck except for the fact that she's got my cock wrapped between her lips. Before I can think or do anything, she's going all the way, though.

That left thumb trick, no gag reflex, and... yeah...

I grunt out in pleasure as my cock slides into the back of her throat. I can feel her tongue all the way on the underside of my shaft, then more, almost to my balls. She's basically got my entire cock in her mouth, but not quite. I help her a little, because I'm a nice guy like that. My fingers wrap into her hair and I pull slightly, getting her the rest of the way.

Don't get me wrong, Ashley is beautiful as fuck. I love her no matter what. She's just extra fucking beautiful when she's got my entire cock in her mouth, the head pressing against the back of her throat, her eyes staring up at me, wide and innocent, Little Miss Perfect Good Girl over here, deepthroating my shaft.

Her eyes start to tear up a little and she squeezes the back of my thigh with her right hand. I let her go and she eases back. I think she's going to take a breather, but she surprises me by going back down again. Not all the way this time, but fast and quick.

She's really fucking good at this. Maybe she's a little too good. I seriously just want to ignore everything and explode in her mouth right now, but what kind of boyfriend would I be then? Even a bad boy has morals. I don't think Ashley knows what kind of monster she's awoken here, but she's about to find out.

Mia Clark

7 - *Ashley*

I DID IT! YES!

I know this is sort of a stupid thing to get excited about, but I feel really accomplished right now. Also, I really like the way Ethan looks at me when I do this. I like when I take his cock in my mouth and I look up and see him looking down at me. He always has this sort of glazed, glossed over look in his eyes. I can see every muscle on his torso, his abs and his pecs, even his shoulders a little bit, and they tense up, flex, and ripple every time I bob up and down, taking him in my mouth, wrapping my lips around his cock.

I like how he squirms a little when I move my tongue, sliding it around his shaft. It's really really sexy, and I like that it's me that makes him move like that. It's exciting to have control over his body this way, even if it's a weird sort of control and a weird sort of excitement.

The best is the sound he makes, and how his muscles get even tighter, flexing as hard as he can, when I take him all the way in. It's not something I can do all the time, and I can probably only do it because of the thumb squeeze trick he showed me and the position we're in right now, but it's a lot of fun. I think Ethan would agree, too.

He practically thrashes as I go all the way down, taking all of him in my mouth. Almost all of him, at least, but he helps me the rest of the way. It makes me smile a little, but it's sort of hard to smile with his cock as far into me as it can possibly go. I feel the slightly sweet, slick trickle of his precum touching against the back of my throat when I have him all the way inside me.

I did it! Yes!

He lets me go when I can't hold him in anymore, and I ease back, but take him into my mouth again just as quick. I guess this surprises him, because his hips buck to meet my lips and he lets out a groan of pleasure. His cock twitches hard and throbs in my mouth.

Oh, is he close? Hm... I kind of want him to cum right now. I kind of want to have sex, too, but I kind of like the idea that he's so excited that he can't help himself.

Ethan is certainly excited, but apparently he still plans on helping himself... to me.

He pulls me up quick before I can protest and spins me around. He grabs my hands and lifts them above my head, pressing my palms against the tiled shower stall walls, then he jerks his hips forward, trying to thrust inside of me. His cock slides between my thighs, not quite penetrating me. He pulls back and pushes forward again. This would be easier if he used his hands, but he seems too far gone to be rational right now.

I like it. Oh my God I love it. I like the feeling of him sliding between my thighs, rutting against me, trying to fill me, but then every time he misses he tries even harder the next time. I can feel his pubic bone and his hips sliding against the curves of my ass while his thighs smack against the back of my legs.

I fidget and squirm, angling downward, arching my back, just so, and the next time he thrusts he fills me perfectly and completely. His cock slides past my lower lips and in a fraction of a second he's all the way in. He grinds hard against my body, his sexual fury temporarily sated. I don't think he's going to be satisfied with this for long, though...

We fuck and I love it. He lets go of my hands, but I keep them raised above my head, pressing them tight against the shower wall. I use my hands for balance, bracing myself for each and every one of Ethan's strong, powerful thrusts. He grabs my hips and pulls me against him with each heavy pound, rattling and shaking directly into my core. The slick water around us and the slickness of my arousal makes it easy for him to take me and to slide his entire length deep inside of me.

Ethan squeezes my hip hard, his fingers pressing roughly into my soft skin, almost painful, but exciting, too. His other hand slips around to the front of my body, pressing against the bottom of my stomach, but then a little lower. His fingers tease and tempt me, rubbing at my clit. He pulls me back onto him while he thrusts hard inside of me from behind and strokes my clit in the front.

I move with him. When he pulls me back, I press my hips back, too. When he pulls out of me, I move forward a little, ready and waiting for his next insistent thrust. My palms press hard against the wall of the shower, but the hot water and steam makes it too slick to really hold onto. My hands keep sliding down even though I try to keep them up. Eventually I settle with keeping them closer to shoulder level near my face, by my cheeks.

Steady, dominant, Ethan leans down and bites lightly onto my neck. I tilt my head back, gasping out a moan. Oh... yesss... I want this. I really really want this. I wanted it this morning, but we were so rudely interrupted, and I can't exactly blame his dad since we shouldn't have been doing *what* we were doing *where* we were doing it, but it doesn't change the fact that I think we both really need this right now.

I hear something soft and distant, but I can't tell exactly what it is. It sounds kind of close, but similar to everything else around us.

"Someone else is in the other shower," Ethan says, whispering into my ear. "You better fucking cum for me soon, Princess. We don't have all day."

Yes, well... *yes*.

"Soon," I whisper to him. "Please, just..."

Ethan knows. He knows a lot, and this is his area of expertise. He shifts his body, angling his thrusts so that they press slightly different inside of me. A slight difference can make all the difference in the world, though. I nearly pass out from the sudden change, the sensation making my entire body reel. As if that isn't enough, Ethan strokes closer and closer to the center of my clit, the tip of his finger light and rough, heavy and soft.

It's us. It's everything we are. Good girl and bad boy, soft and sweet, and rough around the edges. They say opposites attract, and if that's the case, um... we're completely magnetic. Whenever Ethan and I give in to our attraction, we become undone, gone, entirely wrapped up in one another like magnets stuck together. I can't get away from him, and even if I could, I wouldn't want to.

My orgasm surges inside of me. My body tenses and I nearly fall to the ground from the force of it. Ethan holds me up, but my hands slide down. He pulls me back, his hand on my hip moving up towards my breasts, squeezing my nipple, while his other hand continues to tease and toy with my clit. I'm standing there now, unable to control myself, my entire body trembling in slick, warm ecstasy.

Ethan thrusts hard into me one final time, then gives in to his own release, too. His warm, sticky seed fills me, splashing hard inside of me. I feel his cock squeeze and jerk and throb, and I tense and clutch around him as my orgasm takes control of me.

This is all well and good and nice, and honestly I kind of just want to stay like this forever, basking in the warm afterglow of our erotic shower encounter, but then someone calls out to us.

I guess they don't call out to *us* exactly, but he calls out to Ethan.

"You sure are taking your time in the shower, aren't you?" Ethan's dad says, teasing.

He's in the shower stall opposite us. That's why the other shower is on. It's Ethan's dad. Oh my God, can he hear us? Did he hear us? What does he think? That Ethan just found some random girl on his way to the shower and brought her in here to have sex with her?

No. No, calm down, Ashley. I breathe, trying to relax, trying not to burst into anxious hyperventilating.

Ethan presses hard into me once more, his cock twitching and jerking. I think this is more of an angry, annoyed sort of thrust than a sexual one, but it still stirs something deep inside me. It's weird, what with the nervous butterflies crashing around my stomach and the afterglow of my orgasm, plus Ethan's cock still in me, but, um... it's not exactly unpleasurable, but just awkward?

How could it *not* be awkward? Ethan's dad is in the shower right next to us!

"What the fuck," Ethan says to me, muttering under his breath. Louder, to his dad, he says, "Can't blame me for enjoying a nice morning shower, can you?"

I freeze, unsure what to do. Not deterred, Ethan pulls out of me a little, then presses back in. He just came, but he still seems more than excited enough to continue. I bite my bottom lip, entirely unsure how I feel about this.

I kind of want to continue, too. I mean, we both just had wonderful orgasms, but do you know what's better than a wonderful orgasm? Two wonderful orgasms, of course. It makes sense. It is simple math, and I get pretty good grades in math, so I'm positive this is how it works. I think my math teachers would agree, though I don't think I could ever pose this question to them.

The thought of it makes me giggle a little, nervous and excited.

Ethan claps his hand over my mouth and bites onto the back of my neck in warning. I don't know if he realizes this, but it's incredibly erotic.

Ethan's dad is still talking. I couldn't hear what he was saying before, because my thoughts were focused on Ethan's cock inside of me, but um... I really should pay attention here.

"I had a talk with your stepmother," Ethan's dad says, casual, like this is the most normal thing in the world. I don't know if that's true, but I guess maybe? Ethan must shower with the other football players at school after games or whatever, so maybe it's just a man thing? Men like to talk to each other while they take showers, I guess?

I've never showered with other women. Honestly, that seems a little weird. If I'm being extra honest, the idea of Ethan showering with a bunch of other muscular men in close proximity is kind of sexy, though. Um... did I really just think that?

This isn't me talking. It's my libido. I blame Ethan. Mostly I blame Ethan's cock, because he's still inside of me and he's just sending my thoughts into very bad places. Or very good places, depending on how you look at it. This is all his fault.

"I think we got this camping trip off to a bad start," Ethan's dad continues. "I thought maybe you were being overprotective of Ashley with the whole Caleb thing, but I did say this was supposed to be a family trip."

"Yeah, exactly," Ethan says, clenching his teeth. Every time he gets angry, he pulls out of me and thrusts back in.

"I'm not saying that has to change, but maybe you should talk to Ashley and see what she wants to do?" Ethan's dad says. "We can still do family things together, but if she wants to go off with him sometimes, that would be fine, right? Honestly, maybe the three of you can hang out together, too. I was thinking about it, and--"

Ethan squeezes my breast hard, practically mashing it in his hand. I let out a slight whimper, and he eases up. His lips kiss the side of my neck and he whispers to me. "Sorry, Princess. I'm a little worked up at the moment."

"This camping trip is about coming closer as a family, right?" Ethan's dad says.

To me, Ethan mutters, "You think we can get any closer than this, Princess?"

I almost laugh out loud, but stop myself at the last second. Ethan helps by holding his hand over my mouth, too. I lick and kiss his palm, and he grins against my neck, kissing me.

"I sort of get what you're saying, Dad," Ethan says. "I just don't know exactly what you're trying to say here."

"Sometimes we need to keep our distance every so often in order to get closer. If we force ourselves to be close, it can damage our relation-ships. We need to *want* to do it. I guess what I'm trying to say is that maybe this would all work better if we did some things as a family during the day, or later at night, or different times on different days, and then the rest of the time we do our own things. Togetherness, but then separation, too."

"Alright, hold up," Ethan says. "You're saying that it's a family trip, but I should let Ashley go off with that fuck and just let him do whatever the fuck he wants with her?"

Without even missing a beat, he pushes hard into me, then pulls out, continuing a rhythm like that. To make matters worse, his fingers go back to teasing and tormenting my clit. Oh no... this isn't good. This really isn't going to end well.

"You don't have to let her do anything, Ethan. She can decide what she wants to do on her own. And if that's what she wants to do, then so be it. I don't think it's that hard to understand."

"Yeah, I get that," Ethan says, thrusting into me again. I really don't know why he's doing this; and by this, I mean trying to make me orgasm again. I'm pretty sure he's going to succeed, and honestly this is incredibly awkward for me.

"I get it," Ethan continues. "What I don't get is why you're so fucking accepting of that, but what if I want to hang out with her? For real, I'm just being straightforward right now, Dad. You keep talking about Ashley and Caleb but she doesn't even know the guy and she knows me. I thought it would be nice to get to know her better."

"Uh... what?" his dad says, sounding confused. "I thought you'd like the idea of being able to go off on your own. Figured you could go find a girl to romance for a week or two. It's not like I'm saying that Ashley's the only one who should be able to have fun. I'm not even saying it has to get hot and heavy, Ethan. This is a weird conversation for me to be having, to be honest."

It's weird for him? I kind of wonder how much weirder he would find it if he realized what Ethan and I were doing, um... ten steps away or so?

"I want to spend time with her," Ethan says, firm. "I don't know if you forgot already or what, but I'm kind of dating a girl now, too. I'm not going to randomly go romance someone else. I'm trying to be serious here."

"That's... that's good," my stepdad says. "I didn't mean anything by it, but I wasn't sure if you were just saying those things before because we were around Ashley and her mother."

"I wasn't," Ethan says. "I'm being serious about wanting to hang out with Ashley, too. I guess I never really bothered before, because I thought she was too good to hang out with me, but I like her and I think spending time with her will help me be a better boyfriend, you know?"

Um... I suppose that's not entirely untrue, right? It makes me smile. Except then I stop smiling, because I'm about to climax. I really don't know what to do right now, but I can't exactly do much, now can I? I'm sort of trapped here! Trapped between a cock and a hard place, I suppose.

I almost laugh at my own joke, but then, um... oh fuck. Ethan hits all the right places, and my body refuses to stop. I clench and squeeze against him, a second orgasm overcoming me. It's smaller than the first, but even more insistent and demanding than before, too. It won't stop, refuses to be stopped, and probably doesn't even know the meaning of stop. This is the bad boy type of orgasm that my mother never warned me about.

Honestly though, I don't think anyone should warn someone away from orgasms like this. They are definitely kind of amazing.

Ethan and his dad keep talking while my body betrays me. I feel Ethan's body betraying him, too. He fills me a second time, almost as if the first time was just a trial run. This is the real deal, I guess. Also super awkward, but oh well. Sometimes life is awkward, isn't it? This is like that, but magnified, extra awkward.

The shower stops, and I belatedly realized we aren't even clean. I'm pretty sure we're the opposite of clean, actually. Without saying anything, Ethan slips out of me and steps to the side, grabbing his roll of quarters and taking four more. He puts them into the shower timer and turns the knob, bringing back the water.

"Just please don't be a dick, alright?" Ethan says to his dad.

I stare at him, gaping, trying not to smile. I almost laugh, but Ethan gives me a look that says I better not even think about it. It's a silly, playful look, too, though.

"Takes one to know one," his dad says, laughing. "I get it, though. I guess I never thought about it, but, yeah, maybe it'd be nice if you and Ashley spent a little more time together. I just figured you weren't on good terms. You two fight a lot when we're home."

"I'm just teasing her," Ethan says. "I think she knows that."

"Maybe," his dad says. "She's not like you, Ethan. Your personality can be a little hard to handle sometimes."

"Yeah yeah," Ethan says, rolling his eyes. "Whatever. I'll ease up, alright? I'll be gentle with Little Miss Perfect."

"I like when you're rough, though," I whisper to him. I hope I sound sexy. Is it weird if I ask Ethan if that sounded sexy?

Ethan gives me a look. It's a dangerous sort of look that seems to say that if we didn't just have sex twice, he'd pin me against the wall and do it again. Instead, he snatches up his shampoo and starts washing my hair.

Really? *Really, Ethan?* He's so weird. I don't understand him at all.

I do kind of like having my hair washed, though. Ooh... yes, that feels wonderful. His fingers massage my scalp and I practically melt in his hands. I think I just had another orgasm, but not a sexual kind. Erotic hair washing orgasm? Is that a real thing or what? I think it must be, because I'm experiencing it right now.

"Well, let's talk to her today," my stepdad says. "We can ask Ashley what she thinks, just be out and open about it. Later, though. I'm not sure where she went, but she and her mom are going to go grocery shopping for us and you and I are going to head to the bait shop. Some mother-daughter and father-son bonding time. What do you say?"

I have an idea. I don't know if this is a good idea. My stepfather wants to know what I think? Um... I'm right here. I can answer him right now. I shift my eyes back and forth, sneaky, and then I open my mouth wide to loudly tell him my answer.

I'm about to. I was really just going to do it, to tell him that I really want to spend more time with Ethan and also we're dating and I love him. I guess it's not exactly the best time or place, but there's no time like the present, right? Um... sort of...

Ethan stops me, though. He claps his hand over my mouth and gives me a dirty look. "Don't you even dare, Princess. I know what you're thinking. Cut that shit out."

I give him a dirty look back and speak with my eyes. I don't know what I'm saying with my eyes, but they're definitely saying something and it's supposed to be a little angry.

Ethan glares at me, then he lets go of my mouth, except then he bites my bottom lip and kisses me hard. Oh my God. Why does he do this to me? He doesn't even play fair. This is the opposite of fair, and I don't like it.

I do kind of like it, actually, but it's still not fair, it's cheating.

"You almost all set in there?" Ethan's dad asks. His shower is off now and we can hear the rustling sounds of him drying off and getting dressed.

Ethan finishes washing my hair and guides me over to the shower to rinse off, then starts washing his own hair.

"Yeah, almost," Ethan says. "I'll meet you back at the campsite, alright?"

"Sounds good," my stepdad says. "See you soon."

8 - Ethan

DON'T EVEN KNOW WHAT I'm doing anymore. If I'm being real fucking honest, I don't know if I ever knew, but at least my life sort of made sense. Wake up, go to class, or not, get some food like lunch or breakfast or holy fuck maybe brunch, and go to some other classes, do homework or something, practice for football, lift weights, and maybe find a girl to romance for a week or two every so often. Not that difficult, right? Pretty easy, actually.

Now, though, it's like... I don't know, what do I do? I can't just wake up anymore. Waking up is the easiest thing in the world, but every time I do it I have to think of how I'm supposed to handle my relationship with Ashley. What if my dad comes upstairs before I'm awake and realizes Ashley isn't in her room and then he comes to my room and she's completely naked in bed with me? How do you even explain that? Fuck if I know.

We're camping now, so I guess we don't even have to try and explain that, but instead we deal with my dad interrupting us in the middle of sexy situations, and also I can't even take a shower without something happening.

It's not like my dad knows. If I had to guess, he doesn't suspect anything. My dad is a smart guy, but he's not exactly suspicious of much. He focuses on what needs to be done, and I think in his mind he's done with focusing on me. What's there to even focus on? I'm an adult, and I can handle myself, or something like that.

No clue why he keeps harassing me about dating seriously, then, but whatever. Maybe there's something more to that and he doesn't feel comfortable telling me. Yeah, well, guess what, Dad? I don't feel comfortable telling you I'm dating and fucking my stepsister, either, so I'd say we're even.

Once I finish showering, I dry off and get dressed. I give Ashley a quick kiss, except this turns into a not so quick kiss, and then we're just making out in the shower stall. I'll need to remember this for later. If all else fails, we can get some temporary privacy in the shower stall. Sort of, maybe, except there's bound to be other people showering and it's not like we can spend every waking moment in here, even though I kind of wouldn't mind if the opportunity arose.

I'd rather come up with some alternatives, but sometimes you have to take whatever opportunity is presented to you. Comes with the territory of being a bad boy, I guess. Makes life a little more exciting most of the time, too.

We separate, because this has to end. I can't just stay in here making out with her because sooner or later I'm going to want to stay in here and have sex with her, too. Again. We've already done that, but I want to do it again. A lot.

"Hey, calm yourself," I say, stepping back when she grabs for my cock through my pants. "We've got to stop."

She pouts and looks cute as fuck and makes this little whimper whine sound, and I literally almost rip her shorts down her legs and bend her over right then and there. I stop, though. This is like bad boy zen monk shit right here. I am at peace with my inner self, at least for a couple seconds. I better be gone from here before my zen runs out or I'm fucked. Or I guess Ashley would be fucked, but let's just not even start with the double entendres.

"Can I see you later?" she asks.

I laugh. "Where do you think I'm going to go, Princess? Of course you'll see me later."

"Um... I meant... can I *see* you later," she says, staring pointedly down and between my legs.

"We'll figure something out," I tell her. "I don't know what."

"Did you mean what you said to your dad?" she asks, surprising me.

"Huh?"

"About wanting to spend time with me," she says. "Did you mean that? Not just sex."

"What kind of question is that?" I ask her. "Yeah, of course I meant it. Sort of comes with the territory, doesn't it? We're dating, so it makes sense that we should kind of hang out and not just have sex all the time. Don't get me wrong, I love that, too, but, uh..."

"I know," she says. "I just... you shouldn't feel obligated, alright?"

"Obligated to do what? I think I'm pretty fucking obligated here."

She smiles at me and kisses me quick on the cheek. "I meant that I like that you want to spend time with me doing fun things, too," she says. "I know that shouldn't really be a surprise, but it just makes me happy."

"Yeah, well..."

Fuck. How do I explain this? I don't know. I'm not even sure I should try, because I'm pretty sure I'll say something dumb. Dating is hard, alright? Maybe you think it's hard to actually get someone to start dating you, but I think that's the easy part. It doesn't matter if you fuck it up, because you can just move on to the next girl. When you're actually dating, though, it's like... shit, I can't fuck this up. I can't say something stupid, because it's not as easy as just moving on to the next girl.

I don't want to move on to the next girl. I want to stay right here with this one.

"I know neither of us has really done this before," I say to her. "I get that maybe in the past you didn't really have the opportunity to meet guys that weren't complete dicks, and I also get that in the past maybe I seemed like a complete dick, but this is me now, and it's you here, and I love spending time with you, Princess. I like how you're cuddly as fuck, and also sexy as fuck, and cute as fuck, intelligent as fuck, and..."

"I like how you're considerate as fuck," she says, grinning. "Also, I like how you're handsome and sexy and nice, and you're patient and kind, and careful... as fuck."

"Whoa, you're stealing my swag here," I tell her, grinning. "What's with the swearing, too? I thought you were Little Miss Perfect, the one true good girl."

"Oh yeah?" she says, challenging me with her eyes. Fuck, she's beautiful. "Well, I'm pretty sure that bad boys don't like to cuddle, Ethan. I'm pretty sure!"

"The fuck they don't!" I say.

Also, because I really need to stop this, because the urge to have my cock deep inside her is rising with every passing second, I take a step back, then another, and finally I unlock and open the shower stall door. I don't know if I want to fuck her or have sex with her or make love with her, or some combination of the three, but I want to do things to this girl that I seriously don't have time for at the moment.

"I'm going now," I tell her. "Stay in here for a couple of minutes just in case, then head back. I think my dad and I will be--"

She interrupts me with a kiss. Running up to me, she puts her hands on my hips and stands on her tiptoes, kissing me on the lips. Blushing, she sneaks back into the shower stall and stands there, shy. Fuck, she's going to kill me with sexy cuteness. I'm pretty sure I'm done for. The death of a bad boy right here. Woe is me. This is some serious Shakespearian tragedy shit or something.

"Can you take my clothes back?" she asks, holding them out.

"You're stalling," I tell her. "Stalling in the shower stall. I guess this is the best place for it, huh?"

She rolls her eyes at me, then scampers over and stuffs her old clothes in my bag. I totally forget my stuff, was going to just leave it hanging there. She distracts me too much. I can't concentrate on anything but her when she's around.

She brings me my bag and I take it, then I'm gone. I step away before I change my mind and before I do something dumb. She closes the door behind me and hides out while I head back to our campsite.

As I'm passing by the main office, I spot the owner's son out of the corner of my eye. He looks over at me, but when he sees me looking back at him, he turns away.

Yeah, good. Keep your distance, bro. Caleb or whatever the fuck your name is. Yeah, alright, I do actually know his name, but I just don't want to admit it or accept it. He's not important to me. I don't want him to be important to me, and I especially don't want him to be important to Ashley, either.

I just want this trip to go smoothly. As smoothly as it can go, at least. I guess it's already off to a rocky start what with my dad and him not knowing and all of the rest of this shit, but for real, Caleb isn't helping. I'm sure he's a nice enough guy, but if he so much as looks at Ashley with lust in his eyes, I'll kick his ass.

Mia Clark

9 - *Ashley*

I WAIT IN THE SHOWER STALL for a few minutes. It's really very large, all things considered. Since I have nothing else to do, I walk from one end to the other. It's about five or six regular steps wide. You could probably easily shower with four people in here, though I don't know why anyone would want to do that. I definitely liked the two person shower that Ethan and I just shared, though.

I sit on the bench opposite the showerhead wall and wait. I don't have a watch or my phone, because we left everything back home, so I don't know exactly how much time has passed, but I think it's better to wait a little longer to be safe. Just in case, right? In case of what, though?

I guess in case Ethan's father comes back. I don't know why he would, but if he saw me in the shower and he knew Ethan was in here, and I'm obviously done showering, um...

There's no hair dryer in here, so my hair is wet. Ethan's hair was practically dried when he left, since it's so short, but I'm not nearly as lucky as that. I tried to dry it off as best I could with his towel, because I forgot my own, but it's still pretty obvious that I've showered.

What if his dad found out, though? I tried to tell him, or at least I thought about telling him when he was talking to Ethan from the shower earlier, but Ethan stopped me. I know it's something he wants to tell his dad on his own, and I understand that, but I want him to know that he doesn't have to do this all on his own, either. A relationship is two people, isn't it? We can do it together and I can help him if that's easier.

I don't know if it's easier, but I want Ethan to know it's an option available to him.

The drip drip drip of the showerhead distracts me and I fall into daydreaming, remembering things. I remember the feeling of Ethan inside of me, and I remember the touch of his hands on my head, washing my hair. I remember the taste of his lips when I kissed him goodbye. I remember and I love all of it.

I think it's time to go now, or at least I should be able to step out of the shower. I open the door and walk into the open, sunny air. Just because I'm curious, I walk over to where Ethan's dad must have been showering before. There's the bathrooms between our stall and his, but they're still pretty close.

I can't believe Ethan did that! Just... just kept going while he was talking to his dad. It made me nervous, but kind of excited, too. We could have been caught. Maybe not. I don't know how his dad would have caught us, but what if we didn't know he was there? What if we said things in the heat of the moment or if Ethan smacked my butt while he thrust inside of me, or I moaned too loud, and then his dad heard and found out and realized what was going on?

Um... maybe I shouldn't think about that, because I'm pretty sure it would have been bad.

While I'm staring off and daydreaming about silly things, someone comes up beside me.

"Hey, Ashley."

"Oh my God!" I jump and crash into him. It's Caleb.

He falls and I fall on top of him. We land in a heap of awkwardness and arms and legs. I think, um... oh no.

I really didn't mean to and I don't think this is very sexy, regardless, but when I fell on him my hand landed in his crotch. Which, judging by the look on his face, is more painful than pleasant. Except my hand is still there and, um...

I pull it away, and roll to the side, then stand up quick, nervous and confused.

"You really have a bad habit of scaring me," I tell him.

"Sorry," he says, mumbling. "I didn't mean to."

He stands up and brushes the dirt from his pants, back to front and then the sides. I look down without thinking.

"Are you alright?" I ask.

"Yeah, just a fall," he says. "I'm fine."

"I meant, um... your..."

Oh my God, what am I doing? Staring at his crotch, for one, which is not what I want to do. I'm just trying to make sure he's... what? This really doesn't sound good. It seemed innocent enough in my head, at least at first, but when I think about it more, I'm basically asking him about his cock. That's not something you ask someone about! Even if that was something you could ask someone, what am I even supposed to say after that? Oh, do you want me to kiss it better?

Um, no!

Caleb blushes, apparently realizing what I was asking him, and he shifts and fidgets, looking away. It's kind of cute in a fun way. It sort of reminds me of myself, I guess?

"I didn't mean it like that," I say to him. "I'm not very good at this, I don't think."

"Good at what?" he asks, confused.

"Flirting?" I say. "Um... I don't mean that. I mean not flirting. I'm not trying to flirt with you, Caleb. That's what I meant."

"Oh," he says. "Um, alright?"

Good. I'm glad we got that out of the way. That wasn't hard, was it? Is that all there is to it or do I need to say something else so that he doesn't think I'm saying that as a sort of opposite type of thing? Oh, no, is that what he's going to think? That I'm telling him I'm not flirting but in reality that means I really am flirting?

Flirting is difficult. I'm not even trying to flirt and I think I'm accidentally flirting. This is bad. Ugh.

"What are you up to?" he asks.

"I was just taking a shower," I say.

Wait, is that flirting, too? Because I just gave him the perfect reason to imagine me slippery and wet in the shower. I have to stop this.

"I just saw your brother," Caleb says. "Looked like he was taking a shower, too."

"Yup," I say. "We weren't taking a shower together or anything, though. Um..."

I'm really bad at this, aren't I? I don't know what I'm doing anymore.

"Er...?" Caleb gives me a weird look.

"Do you have any siblings, Caleb?" I ask him. I will fix this. I can do it.

"No?"

"Sometimes when you're growing up you end up taking showers or baths together except it's not like that, so don't get the wrong idea, and I'm not saying that Ethan and I did that, but if we did or if you saw anything then it wouldn't be what you're thinking, alright?"

In hindsight, I'm pretty sure I just screwed that up. I thought I was supposed to be smart. Also, I'm technically an only child disregarding my step-brother, so I know absolutely nothing about anything I just said.

"...Alright..." Caleb says.

"It's because Ethan is good at washing hair," I add. "That's all."

"Oh," Caleb says. "Yeah, you've got a lot of hair."

Is that a compliment? Is *that* flirting?

"Thanks," I say. "Well, I've got to go. My mom and I are going grocery shopping."

"Cool," Caleb says. "I'm actually heading there soon, too. Have to pick up a few things. Maybe I'll see you around, then."

Is he asking me on a date? To the grocery store? I'm going to be super honest right now and say that I don't actually know what people do for a first date, but I never considered grocery shopping as an option. It may be one, though. I hope not, because... because.

"Neat!" I say. "Alright, I'm leaving now. Bye!"

I run away. Because. This is awkward. Am I awkward or is Caleb awkward? I... I don't even know.

I head back to the campsite. Quickly!

Ugh.

10 - Ethan

My DAD AND I HEAD OUT in one of the cars as soon as I get back. There's no waiting, no mulling around, just get up and go. Good. I like that. Makes everything easier. We drive through the campground in silence, but stop at the main office to ask the owner something.

I see Caleb there again, but this time he keeps looking at me weird. What's up with this kid? Yeah, yeah, he's probably the same age as me, but he's not even close to my level. He looks kind of scrawny. Alright, I'm willing to give credit where credit is due, and he doesn't exactly look stick thin or anything, but I can tell he doesn't play sports. He's probably in decent enough shape, but that's all the credit I'm willing to give him right now.

I really don't like him. I don't like the way he's looking at me, either, like he's trying to size me up or something? What the fuck?

My dad talks with the campground owner about something or other and I get out of the car, too. Need to show my dominance, you know? Stand tall, make this Caleb kid stay away, or at least be real fucking wary. He should be, too. I know how to throw down when the time calls for it.

"Hey, Ethan," Caleb finally says to me, but his voice is quiet and unsure.

"What's up?" I ask him. Are we friends now or what? I think I missed that memo. Pretty sure I would have ripped it up, too.

"I'm sorry, alright?" he says. "I don't know what your problem is with me, but I'm not trying to cause you any trouble."

"Listen, I don't have a problem with you, but I don't like the way you're staring at Ashley. Got it?"

"I'm not!" he says.

"Yeah, sure. Don't even try to tell me you don't think she's hot."

If he tries to say that, I'll know he's a fucking liar, because, yeah, Little Miss Perfect has some serious sex appeal. She's a little awkward sometimes, and sort of weird, but whatever. That's part of her charm.

Fuck, but then what if he does say she's hot? I'd have to kick his ass, no way around that one. I think I'd have to kick his ass if he says she's not hot, too. That'd be like him calling her ugly, and I can't stand for that.

Except, fuck. Double fuck. I can't kick his ass right here? His dad and my dad are right there, talking. This was part of Caleb's plan, I bet. What a fucking prick. I want to kick his ass even more.

I don't even know why I hate the kid so much. He just... ugh.

"It's just kind of hard to make friends during the summer here," Caleb says. "That's all."

"Yeah? So you thought you'd get friendly with Ashley, is that it?" I know that game. Don't even try to play it.

"No," he says. "I mean, yeah, a little, but you, too."

"What the fuck?" I say. Did he just say what I think he did? "Are you flirting with me, kid?"

"What the fuck, are you serious?" he asks.

I laugh. He finally grew some balls and stood up to me, and it's just kind of funny. He glares at me, but he starts to smile a little, too.

"Ethan, let's go," my dad says. "We've got work to do."

Yeah, well, we're leaving now. I turn away from Caleb and get into the car, simple as that. I'm done talking. What else is there to say?

My dad starts to drive off. We're good. Yeah, this is simple. He got directions to the bait shop and we're heading to get worms or something. Fishing, all of that.

I spare a final glance towards the main campground office and see Caleb sort of looking my way. Not exactly, but he sees me looking back and he does this kind of wave. What the fuck?

I don't know. I wave back, I guess? Polite, that's what that is. A polite wave. Polite as fuck.

Seriously, Caleb is weird. Also he better not flirt with Ashley.

11 - Ashley

I SNEAK THROUGH SOME of the wooded areas instead of following the main road back to our campsite, just in case. I don't want Ethan's dad to see me, and since they're taking the car, they'd drive out and um... maybe see me, so...

It's really not that complicated, but I kind of feel like a stealthy ninja. Sneaky sneaky. I'm not even very sneaky, though. To be honest, I'm kind of clumsy and woods are weird. There's sticks and brush and leaves everywhere and it's hard to move sometimes. I end up half walking, half tripping my way back to the campsite.

Ethan and his dad are gone when I get back, and my mom is there waiting for me. She gives me a suspicious look and a mischievous smile when I return.

"Did you have fun?" she asks.

"Have fun with what?" I counter.

"It seems to me that Ethan left to take a shower, and now that you're back it's obvious you were also taking a shower. Coincidence?"

"Um..."

"You really should be a little more circumspect, dear," my mom says. "It's not that difficult to figure out what you were up to. If your stepfather hadn't left already, he'd probably realize it, too."

"I know, I just... I don't know."

"So when are we going to tell him?" she asks.

"I don't know," I say. "Ethan wants to be the one to tell him, I guess, but also I don't know if we can even tell him, Mom. It's complicated."

She shrugs, nonchalant. "I'm not going to force you or pry, honey. It's your relationship, and Ethan's relationship. You're both welcome to do whatever you want as long as you're not hurting anyone. I would caution that the longer you try to hide this, the more hurt feelings you're going to have to deal with later on."

"I doubt Ethan's dad is going to feel that upset," I say. "I think he'd probably prefer not to find out, actually."

"I don't know. You'd be surprised," my mom says. "It's not him I'm worried about, though. It's you and Ethan. It isn't good to have to sneak around and hide things, especially when those things are a fresh, new relationship that you don't want to hide at all. I worry about you both."

"It's weird, though," I tell her. "Our relationship is weird, Mom."

"It's not that weird, honey," my mom says.

"It's pretty weird! He's my--" I realize I'm being a little loud. I blush and talk quieter. "Ethan's my stepbrother. I don't know why you're so accepting of it, like it doesn't matter. I really appreciate it, but it's still weird, you know?"

"Every relationship is weird, Ashley," my mom says. "How do you think I felt when I started dating Ethan's father? It's hard to date as a single parent, especially when both of us were parents. It's even harder to do when you have children that are older. Not to mention it was confusing and difficult for me at first in other ways, too."

"Why?" I ask.

She's never really talked about this before. We talked about her dating Ethan's dad in the beginning, but to be honest I didn't think it'd go very far. And then, um... it did go far, and they were married, and we moved in with them, so what do I know? Not a lot, apparently.

"Ethan and his father were much better off than us as far as finances are concerned, and as much as I'd like to say that doesn't matter, it really does. When I was alone with him, it was like nothing mattered, but when we went out together, everything changed. When I went to his business parties, I could tell everyone disliked me. They didn't say it to my face, but they whispered about it. Who was I and why was he with me? I was just a single mother trying to survive, Ashley, and in a lot of ways I'm still a mother trying to survive, but I've just added more people to my family now. It doesn't change the fact that people used to wonder why Ethan's father was even bothering with me, and if it was serious or some casual fling, and..."

I've never heard this before. I've never even thought about it. I've always thought of my mom as special, and it's strange to me that anyone could think of her as anything but that. Ethan's dad obviously thinks she's special, and I know Ethan really likes her, too.

It hurts hearing her talk like this.

"We tried to hide it at first, too, you know?" my mom says. "I didn't hide it from you, but we tried to keep our relationship a little more hush hush, but that caused problems of its own. It's not fun to sneak around and make plans based on going somewhere where you know no one will recognize you. We could never really be ourselves unless we were locked away in privacy someplace, but even if we could technically leave and we weren't actually trapped, it still felt like a cage in a lot of ways. I don't want you and Ethan to feel like that, honey. That's the last thing I want you to have to deal with."

"Mom, I..."

I don't know what to say, so I go and hug her instead. She's soft and inviting and I like the way it feels when she puts her arms around me. I've always liked hugging my mom, and I've always felt close to her. I'm not sure why she's never told me these things before, but I'm glad she told them to me now.

"Ethan's dad is lucky to have you," I say to my mom. "I don't care what anyone else thinks."

"Oh, I know he is," my mom says, grinning and teasing me. "I think Ethan is lucky to have you, too."

"I don't know. He's kind of a bad boy." Quieter, whispering, I add, "I think he's corrupting me."

"Oh no, is he?" my mom says, feigning surprise. "This isn't good."

"I kind of like it, though."

"This is very bad," my mom says, shaking her head and letting out an exaggerated sigh. "We'll need to stage an intervention for you."

"I might become a bad girl."

"Actually, you know what?" my mom says. "I think I know how to fix this. We might not need an intervention."

"Oh, how?" I ask.

"S'mores. We'll have to pick up the ingredients for them at the store when we get there."

"What? How are s'mores going to fix anything?"

"How *wouldn't* they?" my mom asks, raising one brow, pretending to look confused. "S'mores solve everything, dear. You'll learn more about it when you're older, but for now you'll just have to trust me."

"I'm kind of an adult, you know? I think I'm old enough."

"That's what they all say, honey. That's what they all say."

I laugh and give my mom another hug. She hugs me back, too. We make sure everything is all set with the campsite, and then we get into the car and head to the store. This is fun. It's like an adventure, but it's more, too. I don't know how to explain it. Just talking with my mom about things makes me feel better. Maybe she can talk with Ethan later, too, and then...

I don't know. She says s'mores solve everything, so maybe we can talk with Ethan's dad tonight and see if it's really true?

12 - Ashley

MY MOM AND I DRIVE up to the main office, but no one's there. A sign on the door says that they'll be back later, with a number to call in case of an emergency. We don't really need to talk to anyone, we just need directions, and there's a bunch of local maps stuffed into a plastic holder on the office door. My mom grabs one and hands it to me.

Thankfully the grocery store is nearby, but it's... strange. To be perfectly honest, I'm not even sure this is a grocery store so much as an expanded convenience store, but I guess it's fine.

We park in the overlarge dirt parking lot, dust settling around the car when we stop. I step out and my mom joins me and we walk to the door. As soon as we open it, a little bell tinkles at the top, sounding our arrival.

A woman standing at the counter on the left greets us as we enter. "Hey there, folks. How's it going?" she says.

"Great!" my mom says. "Oh, isn't this place wonderful?" I'm not sure who she's talking to, but the woman at the counter beams at the compliment. "We're from the city. We're camping a few miles back for the next week or two," she adds, as way of apology or explanation; I'm not sure which.

"Um, I'm going to look around, alright?" I say, mostly because my mom seems intent on staring at the trinkets and doodads hanging on little racks near the counter.

"Oh, sure," she says. "I'll be right there. Take a cart with you and grab anything that looks good. We'll figure out what to have for lunch later."

The carts are miniature versions of what you might find at a regular grocery store, but I guess it's good enough. I take one and march onwards and to the right, which is a small produce section. It's um... very small, though? It makes good use of the size, but everything's cramped and tucked into tall boxes and shelves.

I look through everything, trying to figure out what I'm doing, but to be completely honest I have no idea. It all looks extremely fresh, and according to signs a lot of it is locally grown, which I think is impressive, except I don't really know what I should grab. I pick out a bunch of ears of corn and put them into a plastic bag, then a bushel of berries, some apples, and a small sack of potatoes.

There's fresh strawberries in buckets further down the aisle and I add that to the cart, too. Then, um... I need to see how fresh they are, right? I pluck one out and plop it into my mouth. Oh my God, it's amazing. It's sweet, but a little tart, too, and it just tastes perfect. I chew it and swallow, and then I realize someone's looking at me.

"Um... I was just..." I hope they don't think I was stealing? We're going to pay for these! I have the bucket in my cart and everything.

Oh, it's Caleb. He shakes his head at me and smiles. "There's a trash bucket for the stem right over there," he says, pointing the way.

I hurry over and toss the stem part of the strawberry into the trash, then just sort of look around. I'm not sure what I'm supposed to be doing. Should I talk to him, or just kind of keep going and getting what I need? I don't even know what I need, though. It's not like there's a list, so I'm kind of lacking an excuse to avoid Caleb.

It's not like I want to avoid him, either. I just don't want to flirt with him or give him the wrong idea, except I feel dumb because I don't even know how to do that.

"So..." I say, for lack of anything else to say.

"Sorry," Caleb says. "I'm not following you around or anything. I come here every few days and get stuff for dinner. It's just me and my dad right now. We don't keep a lot stocked, since this place always has fresh food."

"Your mom isn't around?" I ask.

"She's not a big camper," he says.

"Oh, um... you don't all live here?" I ask.

Caleb laughs. "Ha! Can you imagine? It's fun for the summer, but I don't think I'd want to stay here all year round. No, the campground closes down at the end of the season and then we go back home. It's not like home is that far away, though. Two hours or so. My mom comes down sometimes to visit, but she hates the fact that there's no private showers."

"Yeah," I say, smiling. "It takes some getting used to."

"I can help out if you ever--"

I think he realizes what he was just saying, because he stops suddenly and starts to blush.

"I didn't mean, uh... I didn't mean I can help you shower. Er... with the showers. I meant if you need help with anything, just let me know. I..."

I laugh, because it's kind of cute and funny. He really does remind me of myself a little bit, which makes this a whole lot weirder, because I'm not sure how I feel about him now. I think we could be friends, but I'm not sure if, um... is that possible? I don't think Ethan would like that, and also I don't know if Caleb wants that, either. I don't want to give him the wrong impression or anything.

"I should probably just shut up," he says. "I'm sure your brother can help you instead. He seems to know what he's doing."

Oh, yes, he really does, doesn't he? Especially with the showers. A red blush creeps up my cheek as I remember our shower escapades from not that long ago. I don't think Ethan was very helpful with the shower, now that I think about it. We did a lot of non-standard showering activities. Hardly following proper protocol, and I'm not sure how the campground owner would feel about that sort of thing.

Caleb misconstrues my blush, and he blushes even more. "Not that, uh... I didn't mean that, either! I didn't mean that your brother and you... in the shower... er..."

"Caleb, are you trying to flirt with me?" I ask him. I don't think I'd usually be this bold, but dating Ethan kind of makes it easier.

"What?" Caleb asks. I thought he was blushing as hard as he could, but apparently not. His entire face is red now. "No? I mean, I don't think so? Are you flirting with me?"

"What? No!"

"Oh."

A sudden idea comes to mind and I think it's a pretty good one, so I decide to just go with it. "If I tell you something, can you keep it a secret?" I ask him.

"Sure," he says. "What is it?"

"I know my dad said that I broke up with my boyfriend before, but that's not entirely true."

"Oh," Caleb says. "You got back together with him?"

"No, um... I met someone else after that and we're dating but it's kind of a secret. I can't tell anyone yet."

"You can't tell anyone what?" my mom asks, stepping out from an aisle and joining me.

Caleb stands stock still, as if we've both been caught and we're in a lot of trouble now. I guess we would be, except it's just my mom.

"She knows already," I tell him, and he loosens up and breathes a sigh of relief.

"What do I know?" my mom asks.

"About my secret boyfriend," I tell her.

"Ashley!" my mom says, her mouth open in a false show of surprised shock. "You have a secret boyfriend?"

I roll my eyes at her. Caleb stiffens again. He's kind of funny and cute with how awkward he is. It makes me smile.

"I was telling Caleb that I have a secret boy-friend but we can't tell anyone yet."

My mom nods twice. "Ah, yes. Alright."

"Wait, why can't you tell anyone? Why are you telling me?" Caleb asks.

"I think it's more that we can't tell my hus-band," my mom says. "We're not sure if he'd approve yet."

"Yup. Also, I think that's why Ethan's being extra protective," I add.

My mom gives me a curious, sidelong glance. Obviously she knows, but she must have realized I'm not telling Caleb everything, too.

"Does he know your boyfriend?" Caleb asks.

"Oh, yes," my mom says, taking over for me. "Ethan's extremely close with Ashley's boyfriend. They're inseparable, really."

Um... I guess that's true? I don't think Ethan can separate himself from himself, so...

"He's kind of scary," Caleb says. "Is he always like that?"

"Who, Ethan?" I ask, and Caleb nods. "Yup, mostly, but he's pretty nice, too."

"Sometimes," my mom adds, "except when he's not."

"Well, I'm not trying to... to flirt with you or anything. I'm not trying to break up you and your boyfriend," Caleb says, stumbling with his words.

"Maybe you should tell Ethan that?" my mom says.

I give her a look. I don't know what kind of look it is, but I also don't know what she's playing at with this. I think it's my fault since I started all this and I can't exactly blame her for continuing it, but if Caleb says that to Ethan out of the blue, um...

I don't think that's going to go very well. I can tell Ethan beforehand, though. This'll work. This is as good a plan as I can come up with so that we can keep everything a secret and so that Ethan doesn't have to get jealous all the time.

Though, if I'm being honest, I kind of like Ethan when he's jealous. He gets extra protective and a little rough and I really can't complain about the sexy stuff he does. I'm not sure if last night was brought on by his jealousy or just normal bad boy behavior, but I feel like I should leave my options open.

I do want him to know he doesn't have to be jealous. I like when he's a little grabby and possessive, though. Will he still be grabby and possessive when he's not jealous? I'm not sure, but knowing Ethan, yup, probably.

My mom and Caleb are talking about he intricacies of my secret boyfriend, and I feel like I should chime in, so I do.

"You just can't tell anyone, alright?" I say.

"Alright," Caleb says. "I won't. I promise."

"It's just you, me, my mom, and Ethan who knows. No one else does," I say. Jake does, I remember, but... ugh, I'm not even going to think about him. I don't have to for a few weeks, and I plan to take full advantage of that fact.

"Alright," he says again.

"Not even your dad. You can't even tell your best friend in the entire world over the phone, even if I'll never meet them."

Caleb nods. "I swear I won't."

"Alright, good," I say, nodding firm, trying to sound super serious.

My mom nods, too, and scrunches up her brow, her lips pursed, looking super serious, as well.

I'm glad we're all serious here, because I think this plan is either horrible or one of my best yet. Probably not the best, because I kind of think my sexy plans with Ethan are the best, but this is still a good one.

"Do you want to help us shop, Caleb?" my mom asks.

"Is that alright?" Caleb asks.

"Yes," I say. "Just don't try to kiss me or my boyfriend will hurt you."

"Oh, he's not here though, is he?" Caleb asks, then starts blushing again. "I mean, I'm not going to kiss you but I just... I'm sorry. I didn't mean it like that!"

I glare at him a little, lips pursed, trying not to laugh. Caleb is funny, I like him. "He'll know if you do," I say. "He's not here right now, but don't underestimate him. He's kind of a bad boy, and he's not afraid to get into trouble."

"If he's anything like your brother, I believe it," Caleb says.

Yes, well, he's a lot like my stepbrother, actually. Basically exactly like him in every way, because they're the same person, but I'm not going to say that. No one else has to know. Everything will be fine. We'll take this one day at a time, right?

Yup!

"Do they have graham crackers here?" my mom asks.

"Yeah, they're right over here," Caleb says. "Are you going to make s'mores?"

"We are! Oh, what about marshmallows? Chocolate, too. I saw some chocolate bars up at the counter, so we're probably fine there, but if there's anything else, we should weigh our options before we commit."

Caleb smiles and he leads us around the store. We get everything for the s'mores, then some fresh bacon straight from the butcher, chicken breasts, some canned vegetables that weren't available fresh in the produce section, and a bunch more. Not too much, but it should tide us over for the next few days.

While the woman at the counter is ringing us out, I smile over to Caleb. "Do you want to come over tonight for s'mores?" I ask him

"Uh... is that alright?" he says.

"Sure, why not?"

"Er... Ethan? I think he hates me."

"He probably does," I say, faking a frown and nodding.

"Ashley! Ethan does not hate him," my mom says, shocked. "He heavily dislikes him, that's all."

Caleb stands there, mouth open wide, looking at the both of us. He looks a little worried and scared, like as soon as we get back to the camp-ground Ethan is going to search him out and beat him up or something. It's kind of funny but then I feel a little bad, too.

"Ethan doesn't hate you," I say. "I don't think he does. I'll talk to him, alright? Just don't try to flirt with me or kiss me."

"You should probably avoid hugs or overly friendly gestures, too," my mom adds.

"What kind of overly friendly gestures?" Caleb asks. "How do I know what to do?"

"You probably shouldn't smile or laugh," my mom says. "Also, I'd suggest standing at least arm's length away from Ashley at all times. Don't look at her for more than two seconds, either."

"Are you serious?" Caleb asks.

"No, not particularly," my mom says, grinning.

Caleb stares at her like she has two heads. I think it might be an apt assessment at the moment. My mom really seems to like teasing him. It's kind of funny. I start to laugh, and Caleb shuffles side to side for a second before cracking a smile.

"You'll be fine, dear," my mom says, patting him on the shoulder. "Just be yourself, alright? We'd love to have you over for s'mores later. It'll be fun."

13 - Ethan

THE BAIT SHOP IS CRAZY. I don't mean to sound like some spoiled city kid, but they seriously have taxidermy stuff in here, too. It's not a bait shop so much as an all-purpose outdoorsman sort of place. There's guns locked up in cases behind a counter, and archery equipment off to the side, plus more fishing rods than any one person could ever need. The guy who runs the place does taxidermy too, I guess, and he's showing my dad his handiwork.

I'm not sure if my dad is impressed or scared. I feel like in a situation like this you should be a little bit of both. You don't want to screw around with a guy who makes home decorations out of dead animals. I have to admit, they do look pretty cool, though. There's a large moose head on a plaque hanging high up on the wall behind the clerk's counter. That is not a moose I'd want to mess with.

Also, there's a bear. An entire bear. It's standing on two legs on a short wooden pedestal, paws stretched out like it's about to attack you. I'm pretty sure if Ashley saw it, she'd faint. It's cool, Princess, I'll catch you. I'm your knight in bad boy armor or something.

Just so you know, the bear isn't real, though. The taxidermy guy made sure to tell me that. They aren't allowed to shoot bears here. I guess if you see a bear you just punch it or something? Or you hope and pray you never see a bear to begin with. Fuck if I know?

I go to a cooler in the back and look through my options while my dad talks with the shop owner. Let's see, for fishing we have... worms, worms, and worms. Lots of choices. I go with the worms on the right instead of the worms on the left, because who the fuck likes things on the left? I don't know. Actually, I have nothing against left as a direction, but I just felt like going with the worms on the right.

I take them over to where my dad and the shop owner are talking, but before I get there I see John, the campground owner.

"Hey," he says to me, smiling and waving.

I wave back. "Hey."

"You all going fishing later?"

"Probably not today but we brought fishing poles, so we might try at the lake," I say.

"Nice," John says. "Yeah, it's fun. You could try the river, too. Feeds into the lake, but you can catch different kinds of fish over by there sometimes. They're a little more feisty if you're looking for a challenge." He winks at me.

I don't know why he winks at me, but I guess I look like someone looking for a challenge? I'm fine with it, because it's probably true. Who wants to do easy stuff? Yawn, boring.

"Caleb knows his way around there and he loves fishing if you want to ask him," John says. "He gets kind of bored hanging out at the campground all day, so he'd love an excuse to take off for awhile."

"Yeah, maybe," I say, gritting my teeth. Do I look like I want to hang out with Caleb? I guess so, if his dad just said that, but whatever. "Is he here?"

"Nah, he went to get food. He's at the grocery store."

Wow. Seriously? I guess this could be a coincidence, but I don't know. He just coincidentally goes to the grocery store when Ashley and her mom are also coincidentally going to the grocery store, and that little fuck is going to have a chance to be alone with her now? Seriously, what the fuck bullshit is that? Obviously I'm not there, either, and that pisses me off, because who knows what he's saying?

I bet he thinks he's smooth and suave, too. Talking some crap about wanting to lay out under the country sky and look at the stars with her or something. Let's go into the woods. It's magical. Also, take your pants off and let's fuck.

I really don't like him. Only I'm allowed to tell Ashley to take her pants off so we can fuck. I'm pretty sure one of the perks of being a boyfriend is that you get to say stuff like that. I mean, I don't know for sure, but I'm just pretty sure that's one of the perks. Feel free to correct me if I'm wrong.

The stars and shit, too. Only I'm allowed to ask her to look at the stars. Why the fuck didn't I ask her if she wanted to look at the stars yet? Fuck. I'm not good at this boyfriend thing. I need to step up my game here.

Fuck you, Caleb.

"Are you alright?" John asks me, looking at me funny.

"Yeah, I'm fine," I say, frustrated. "Just can't fucking wait to go fishing, that's all."

Yeah, that's it. Makes sense, right?

I guess so!

"Ah," John says, giving me an understanding nod. "I know what you mean. There's nothing quite like the sense of calm and relaxation that comes over you when you first cast your line. It's truly amazing."

"Yeah," I say, trying not to laugh. He sounds so into it. Fishing is pretty nice, though.

"I'll tell Caleb you might want to go," he says. "I've got to head out, though. Let me know if you all need anything back at the campground, alright?"

"Sure," I say.

I decide not to add that I need his son to stay the fuck away from Ashley. I mean, he asked if I needed anything, and I think that kind of counts, but maybe it's not the best thing to say.

I head over to my dad and the taxidermy guy. They're looking at a fish now. I don't know why anyone would ever do that to a perfectly good fish, because it looks like it would have made a great dinner, but whatever. Apparently you can taxidermy a fish. What the fuck, is that even what it's called? *Taxidermy?*

"Worms!" my dad says as I join him. "Great."

"Did you want to get some of that deer jerky I mentioned, too?" the shop owner asks him. "It's as fresh as it gets. Genuine country flavor and I smoke it at home myself."

Holy fuck, deer jerky? Seriously, that sounds amazing. I guess I'm drooling or something, because both my dad and the shop owner seem excited by the look on my face.

"You think we should get some for the ladies?" my dad asks.

"Yeah, but I don't think we should tell them it's locally made. They're going to think it's Bambi's mother or something."

My dad laughs. This is kind of nice, just hanging out with him. I wish we did it more often.

That's what the camping trip is for, though, right?

Yeah, maybe. Hopefully.

Mia Clark

14 - Ashley

B Y THE TIME MY MOM AND I get back to the campsite, Ethan and his dad are already there. They're just mulling around, goofing off, and it's kind of nice to see. I know Ethan and his dad don't always see eye to eye, and sometimes his dad doesn't have a lot of free time outside of work, but I think Ethan wishes they could spend more time together.

I don't know why I think that. I haven't actually ever really talked with Ethan about it before. It's just something I've thought about sometimes. I like spending time with my mom, and I honestly couldn't even imagine *not* spending time with her. I call her every day when I'm at college and tell her almost everything. I know Ethan doesn't feel as comfortable as that with his dad, but...

I don't know. Maybe he wants to be? Even if they aren't, I think it would be nice if he at least felt like he could be comfortable talking with his dad about things.

I suppose I have ulterior motives there, because I want him to tell his dad about us, but that's not the only reason. I'm just not sure what the other reasons are yet.

"Well, hello there, boys," my mom says after we park and get out of the car. "What kind of trouble are you two getting into?"

"We grabbed some jerky at the bait shop. Want to try some?" my stepdad asks.

Ethan's already eating his own piece. He spares a glance over at me while his dad comes to offer my mom some jerky.

"Ashley?" he asks, holding the bag out for me, too. "It's good stuff."

I take a small piece and try it. Oh, wow! It really is pretty good. I chew and swallow, and I kind of want another piece, but Ethan's dad is hanging around my mom by the firepit now. He also has the bag of jerky. Ethan sees me staring and he steals a piece for me and brings it over.

I smile. "Thanks."

"Yeah, no problem," he says. Then... "Meet anyone interesting while you were shopping?"

"Huh?"

"Caleb?"

"Oh." Um... this doesn't look good. Ethan looks kind of mad, actually. "Yup, he was there," I say, trying to sound casual and nonchalant. I'm not sure if it works.

"And?" he asks.

"I don't know. He was just there," I say. It's not like I can explain everything to him right now. "He helped me and my mom with our shopping. He had to buy some things, too."

"Yeah, sure," Ethan says, rolling his eyes. "I'm sure that was it."

I stick my tongue out at him. "Well, that really *was* it. You don't have to be jealous or anything."

Ethan gives me a look, and it's a kind of sexy, smoldering look, though I'm not entirely sure what it's for. I kind of want to find out what it's for, though.

He sneaks closer to me and whispers something.

"Um... what?" I say, confused.

"Just do it," he says.

Ugh. I don't know what he has in mind, but I'm pretty sure nothing good will come of it. I'm curious, though. This is a dangerous combination, the demanding bad boy and the curious good girl, but I think I can handle myself now. If not, I'm sure I'll enjoy what Ethan has in mind, so...

"I have to go to the bathroom," I say to Ethan's dad and my mom. They stop looking lovingly at each other and look over at me. "I'm just, um... I forget how to get there?"

Ethan grumbles. He's not even grumbling, though! He's pretending to grumble. What a jerk, seriously.

"Yeah, yeah," he says. "I'll show you. Try and remember, though. I don't want to have to do this every single time you've got to go."

I glare at him and stick my tongue out. My mom laughs, but my stepdad just rolls his eyes at the two of us. Alright, good, this is sort of going according to plans, I think.

"Ethan, stop teasing her," my stepdad says. "Ashley, it's fine. I can show you if you want, and Ethan and your mom can stay here and start making lunch?"

"Nah, it's cool," Ethan says, grabbing my arm. "Come on, Princess. I'll show you."

I know where the bathrooms are, though. They're up front by the main office, which is kind of far away but not that far. I can get there fine on my own, but Ethan told me to make it seem like I couldn't, so, um... well, we're going together now.

I don't even have to go to the bathroom, either. Also, as soon as we're out of view of our campsite, Ethan takes a serious detour.

He guides me a little further into the woods, going directly away from the bathrooms. I follow, partly because I'm curious and mostly because I'm a little excited at how excited Ethan seems. He might not show it very well, but I can feel the anticipation in his fingertips, the slight squeeze as he holds my arms, and his quick pace as we hurry to hide in the woods.

It's not like we're that far away, but we move off the beaten path and hide behind some trees. We're effectively hidden now, or mostly hidden. I doubt anyone will see us.

Ethan spins around, then pushes me against one of the trees, pinning me there with his body. He grabs my hips and moves close, grinding against me.

"Yeah, so, what's up with Caleb?" he asks.

I smirk and toss my hair over my shoulders. "Why?" I ask him. "Are you jealous?"

"Yeah, actually, I kind of am," Ethan says.

"Oh." I laugh because I didn't expect that.

"Yeah, real funny, Princess," Ethan says, smirking. "Seriously, though, why'd he follow you to the grocery store? I don't like that kid."

"He's not even a kid," I say. "He's the same age as us. If he's a kid then I'm a kid and you're a kid, too."

"Yeah, yeah, whatever."

"He just had to go shopping, that's all," I say. "He told me he was going when I left the shower earlier but you and your dad were gone by the time I got back to the campsite so I couldn't have told you. Honestly it's not a big deal."

"Wait, he was stalking you outside the shower, too?"

"Ethan," I say, exasperated. "The front office is right by the showers and the bathrooms, so it makes sense that he would be there."

"Yeah, I guess," Ethan says, scrunching up his brow. "I saw him there, too, so maybe he's not stalking you."

"I think you're stalking me," I say, lifting my chin up and sticking my tongue out at him. "What do you say to that?"

Ethan rolls his eyes at me, then he kisses me quick. I gasp and look around, but no one's nearby and I don't think anyone can see us here either way. This is a pretty good hiding spot, actually.

"Listen," Ethan says. "He doesn't seem like such a bad guy, but I don't like the way he looks at you."

"It's not like you can stop him from looking," I say, shrugging a little.

"You want him to look?" Ethan asks, confused.

I sigh. "No. I'm just saying that he knows I have a boyfriend now, so whether he looks or not, it doesn't matter. I told him he can't flirt with me or kiss me."

"Wait, hold up. Did he try to kiss you or flirt with you? What the fuck?"

"No!" I laugh. Ethan looks so concerned and serious. "Ethan, the only thing that happened is my mom teased him a lot and he helped us buy groceries. He might come over later and have s'mores with us, too."

"Fuck," Ethan says, muttering. "I don't like that."

"It's just s'mores," I say, trying to sound casual. I mean, it's mostly casual, but it's a little hard to sound casual when I'm pinned against a tree with Ethan pressed hard against me. I kind of want to do less than casual things at the moment.

"Wait a second, you told him you had a boyfriend? Did you tell him about us?"

"Oh. No. I just, um... I told him it was a secret, and that I had a secret boyfriend. My mom went along with it. Now you don't have to worry, right? I told him he can't tell your dad, too. You won't have to worry about him trying to flirt with me or anything now."

"I guess," Ethan says, shrugging.

"You guess?" I ask. "Why'd you want me to say I had to go to the bathroom, anyways?"

"Oh, you want to know, do you?" he asks with a sneaky bad boy grin.

"I don't know, do I?" I counter.

Ethan answers, but he doesn't play fair. He wraps my hair around his fingers, pulling slightly, then he kisses me hard. I gasp from the sudden surprise, but then I move into his kiss. I try to move into it at least, but Ethan *really* doesn't play fair. Whenever I try to kiss him harder, he squeezes slightly and pulls me back with his hand in my hair. His other hand is... um... also not playing fair.

"We're out in the open!" I hiss at him, squirming and trying to get away.

I can't go anywhere, though. Um... I'm kind of pinned to a tree here? Send for help?

Ooohhh, nope! Nevermind, I don't need help! I'm good! I'm fine. Mmmhmmm, really really good and fine and wonderful...

Ethan unbuttons my shorts with one hand and shoves his hand down the front. He slips past my panties and cups at my sex while kissing me hard and grabbing my hair. Oh my God, I seriously can't believe he's doing this.

I also can't believe I'm letting him. I'm supposed to be the good girl here, aren't I? Except I don't have a choice! That's what I'm telling myself, at least. He's kidnapped me and is ravaging me in the middle of the woods against my will.

I'm pretty sure if I did have a choice I would choose this, though. It'd be an easy choice to make, don't you think?

Ethan moves his hand to the back of my shorts and grabs my ass hard, pulling me closer to him. I can feel his growing erection grinding against the core of my body. Inadvertently, I grind against him, too, but then I remember myself and I squirm and try to get away.

"Oh, you want to play hard to get?" Ethan asks.

"I just don't think this is a very good place to do this!" I say, laughing. "What if someone sees us?"

"Who do you think is going to see us?" he asks. "We're in the middle of the woods."

"Um, the main path is literally right over there?" I say, kind of pointing with my eyes. To be honest, I can't see it, because it's behind me and there's a tree in the way, but it's still there. The path is definitely there and someone might be walking down it right now.

"Oh, shit, you're right!" Ethan says, wide-eyed. "Holy fuck, hey, Dad, uh... what's up?"

Oh my God, it's Ethan's dad. My stepfather. My shorts are undone. They are unbuttoned and this close to falling down my... well, there they go. My shorts are around my ankles and I'm standing pinned to a tree with Ethan grinding his half-erect cock against me.

And he still has his hand on my ass! Seriously.

I squirm and try to get away but Ethan just holds me tighter and starts to laugh.

"I don't know--" I struggle against him. "--why you're--" More struggling. "--laughing!"

"It's just a joke, Princess," he says. "Lighten up. No one's there. No one can see us. We're fine. I kind of just want to have a little fun with you, if you don't mind?"

"Do I have a choice in the matter?" I ask him, trying to sound indignant. I don't think it's working very well, because I keep grinding my hips closer to him, and also I try to kiss him.

"Yeah, you've got a choice," he says. "Option A is I fingerfuck you to orgasm right here, or Option B is we go a little further into the woods and see what kind of mischief we can get into."

"Mischief?" I ask. "And what does that entail?"

"Basically involves me pulling aside your panties, pushing you against a tree, and fucking you hard from behind," he says.

I can't even believe he just said that.

"What about Option C?" I ask. "All of the above?"

I can't even believe I just said that.

Ethan seems impressed. "I'm open to the idea," he says. "Kind of excited about starting with Option A, though."

I've given my answer, sort of, and Ethan already has his reply in mind, so...

He squeezes my ass hard and then slips his fingers between my legs from behind, teasing at the bottom of my pussy. I fidget and moan, but he kisses me, keeping me quiet. Without warning, he moves his hand to the front and then plunges a finger hard into me. Oh my God. I didn't even know I was this excited, but... nope, I'm this excited.

He pulls his finger out of me and then brings his hand up. "You're so fucking wet for me, Princess. I love it," he says.

He licks his finger, tasting my arousal, then he gives me a taste, too. Without thinking, I let him stick his finger in my mouth and I suck and tease at it, trying to make it look like I'm sucking on something else entirely.

"I want you--" I say, but before I can finish, he slides his hand between my legs again, playing with the slick folds of my sex. "--inside me!"

"Just calm the fuck down, Princess," Ethan says, grinning. "I want to take my fucking time here and savor this. I didn't get to spend nearly as much time as I wanted with you this morning. Honestly I'm kind of pissed about that, but I think we can make up for it."

"Ohhh, yes, I hope so," I say, gasping as he slides his finger into me again.

I'm not sure what happened after that, but it's nothing good. It's probably the opposite of good, and really really bad, but not in a good way like Ethan's bad boy ways. This is just entirely bad.

"...Ashley?" someone says. I recognize the voice, but it takes me a second to realize who it is. "Is that... oh shit, wow."

It's Caleb. What's Caleb doing here? Oh no. Oh my God. What is going on?

Ethan seems to realize this is really bad, too. I know he likes being a bad boy and doing bad things, but this isn't really the same. He pulls his finger out of me and removes his hand from my panties, then in one swift motion he bends down and pulls my shorts up my legs. I scramble with the buttons and try to act like nothing's going on.

It's kind of hard, because Caleb is literally standing a few steps away, and he just saw every-thing.

"That's... your brother. Oh my God, you were doing... *what*. What's going on? Uh..."

"Nothing," Ethan says, glaring at him. "What the fuck are you doing here?"

I'd kind of like to know the same thing! I feel bad. I don't know why I feel bad, except that I didn't want Caleb to see that. I really didn't want anyone to see that, though. I wish I could just blame Ethan, or myself, or the both of us, and be done with it, but I'm really embarrassed right now.

I blush and mumble and try to think of something to say, but the only thing I can think of is that Caleb just saw Ethan fingering me. It's not like he saw much, because my panties were still on, but it's not like he can't connect the dots and realize what was happening. It's pretty easy to tell what Ethan was doing to me.

"You forgot your strawberries at the store," Caleb mumbles. "I was just... I was just bringing them to you and then I heard something so I came to see what it was, and... Ashley, that's your brother, isn't it? I don't understand?"

"You say a word of this to anyone and you're dead," Ethan says to him. "Got it? That's all you have to understand, kid."

I understand why Ethan is upset, but I think maybe he needs to think about how he sounds, too. I don't realize this until after the fact, but, um...

"No!" Caleb says. He's loud and defiant, standing tall. "I won't let you hurt her. Ashley, was he hurting you?"

Um... no? Not exactly... in fact it was probably the opposite of *hurt*. I really really liked it.

It's sort of hard to say that, or explain it, though. This is complicated. What do I do?

Caleb is loud enough that we're sort of causing a commotion here. A few other campers that were walking down the main road notice us. I spot them talking amongst each other out of the corner of my eye. We're making a pretty big scene now, and it's going to get bigger if we don't do something.

Caleb tries to grab my hand and pull me away. "Come with me. I'll--"

I guess we make an even bigger scene when Ethan pushes Caleb to the ground.

To be fair, I think Ethan wanted to punch him. I don't know this for sure, but I'm really thankful he didn't, because Caleb isn't a fighter. I don't think Caleb has even been in one fight his entire life. Ethan pushes him, and Caleb falls, and that's about it, except there's people watching us and I don't think this is good.

Caleb had the bucket of strawberries in his hand, but they crash to the ground, scattering everywhere. He stares up at me, wide-eyed.

"Ashley..." he says.

"Caleb, it's fine," I tell him. "I... I promise, alright? It's fine? I'll try to explain it to you later, because it's kind of a funny story..." I try to laugh, but it's a little hard right now. "Ethan wasn't hurting me. I wanted to be here. We just got, um..."

I don't know. I can't explain this now. I don't know how to explain it to Caleb, and I especially don't know how to explain it to him with an audience. A few more people have joined the other campers, and I hear someone mentioning they should send for the campground owner. Oh, yes, that's exactly what we need right now. If Caleb's father comes, I'm pretty sure we're all in even more trouble.

"Ethan, come on," I say, tugging at his hand.

He clenches his jaw and doesn't say anything, but he comes with me when I pull him away from the tree. It's the tree I was leaning against while he fingered me just a few moments ago.

Yup, so... this is really awkward...

Ethan and I start to walk off, but before we get very far Caleb calls after us.

"Ashley. Ethan, too. You both better tell me what's going on. I'll come by your campsite later. If you don't come with me and explain this to me, I'm going to tell your parents what I saw."

I try to... to say something. I mumble. The crowd watching us is leaving, and I don't think they saw much of anything except Ethan and Caleb fighting. That's not so bad. Caleb is the one who saw the worst of it, which... yup, that's pretty bad.

"I swear to God, if that fuck tries to blackmail you into some bullshit, I'll kick his fucking ass," Ethan mutters under his breath. "I told you I didn't like him, and it's pretty fucking obvious why now."

"One hour!" Caleb calls out. "I'll come in an hour, alright?"

It just doesn't sound mean, though. I don't know how to explain that, but I don't think Caleb is mean. I don't think he's going to blackmail me. Maybe I'm not a good judge of character, though. Maybe Ethan is right. I thought Jake was nice before, too, and look how that turned out?

Oh my God, what if Caleb tries to do the same thing?

I can't think about that. I don't want to think about that. I hurry with Ethan, hand in hand. We don't go back to our campsite yet, though. We head to the bathroom instead. I think we both need to calm down and cool off a little, and that's the only place we can be alone, at least for now.

An hour? That's it? What am I supposed to do or say?

We can't even do or say anything. It's not like Ethan and I can somehow explain to our parents that we have to leave immediately, that the camping trip we literally just started yesterday, that was supposed to last for at least a week or maybe two, has to come to an abrupt end.

I don't know what to do. What if Caleb does try to blackmail us?

It's embarrassing, but my mom would understand what happened, at least a little bit. She might sigh and shake her head, but she wouldn't get too upset. She might even laugh about it.

Ethan's dad, though... I really don't think my stepfather would understand, and I doubt this is the way we should tell him.

When we get to the bathroom, Ethan lets out a deep sigh. "Fuck," he says. "Let's just run away together. How's Antarctica sound?"

"Cold," I say. "With lots of penguins."

Despite the severity of our situation, Ethan laughs. I laugh, too. He puts his arm around me and hugs me tight.

"I'll just tell him, alright?" he says. "My dad, I mean. I'll tell him if Caleb tries to do something to hurt you. It's probably a really fucking bad time for it and I don't know how he'll take it, but it's better than the alternatives."

"Maybe," I say. "I... I don't know. Ethan, do you trust me?"

He looks into my eyes and nods. "Yeah, of course I do, Princess."

"Let's just talk to Caleb first, alright? Then we can decide what to do from there."

"Are you serious?" Ethan asks. It's obvious by the look on his face that he hopes I'm not serious.

"Please?" I ask him. "Pretty please?"

"Fucking..." Ethan mumbles to himself.

Then, without warning, he kisses me. We're even more in the open now than we were before, but there's no one around. We're in the back part of the shower and bathroom building, mostly hidden by trees and the building itself. If someone steps around the corner, they can see us, but other than that, we're safe.

The kiss doesn't last for long, but it's passionate and sweet and I love it.

"I love you," Ethan says. "I think this is a really fucking bad idea, but I'll trust you."

"I love you, too," I say, smiling at him.

To be honest, I kind of think it's a bad idea, too, but...

I just want Ethan to be able to tell his dad on his own terms. I don't want him to be forced into it. I don't know exactly what I want, but I want Ethan to be happy.

This is the only way I can think of to make that happen.

I hope it's the right decision. I really really hope so.

Mia Clark

A NOTE FROM MIA

EEK... CALEB FOUND OUT, and in the worst way possible...

I'm not sure how this is going to go for Ethan and Ashley. It's kind of bad. Is Caleb going to end up telling Ethan's dad? I'm not sure how Ethan's dad will feel about that, but what are the alternatives here? I guess Ethan can just tell his dad himself, but it seems like their relationship is still a little rocky.

Is Caleb like Jake, though? I don't know... he seems nicer with Ashley, but Ethan obviously has problems with him. He might just try to take advantage of the situation, though. Sometimes it's hard to tell, and like Ashley was saying to herself, sometimes it's hard to judge people at first, especially when you don't know them. Maybe

Ethan really does have a good reason to dislike Caleb. Who knows?

I know, but I can't tell you. It's a secret!

There will be more soon, though, don't worry.

The next book will be here shortly, and it will wrap up a lot. As far as everything is going now, there should be six episodes total for this season, so we're almost at the end. I'm going to add a few extra scenes at the end of the last book just for fun, because camping is fun and everyone should be having fun, though. I promise it'll be fun!

I hope you're liking everything so far, though. I'd love it if you could leave me a review and let me know what you think so far! How do you feel about Caleb? Do you think Ethan's dad is going to be upset, or how is this going to go? I'm nervous!

Bye for now!

~MIA

ABOUT THE AUTHOR

Mia likes to have fun in all aspects of her life. Whether she's out enjoying the beautiful weather or spending time at home reading a book, a smile is never far from her face. She's prone to randomly laughing at nothing in particular except for whatever idea amuses her at any given moment.

Sometimes you just need to enjoy life, right?

She loves to read, dance, and explore outdoors. Chamomile tea and bubble baths are two of her favorite things. Flowers are especially nice, and she could get lost in a garden if it's big enough and no one's around to remind her that there are other things to do.

She lives in New Hampshire, where the weather is beautiful and the autumn colors are amazing.

Made in the USA
San Bernardino, CA
20 November 2019

60194507R00071